PRISON BREAK

The guard carefully sighted his rifle. It was clearly going to be a pleasure to burst Fargo's head like a ripe summer melon. A guard did not often get to have such an honor.

He made one mistake. In taking the time to sight well, he gave Fargo an opportunity to raise his Colt. Fargo had nothing against the man personally, so when he fired it was simply to blast the carbine from the man's hand.

There was something comic about the moment—the guard preparing to fire and then throwing his weapon up in the air as Fargo's bullet ripped across his knuckles. The guard screamed in a high-pitched voice and then sank to his knees. He probably wasn't even in all that much pain. He'd just been shocked by Fargo's surprise move.

Fargo fired twice more above the collapsed man's head so that the guard wouldn't try to stop him as he came hurtling through the open gate. . . .

THE
TRAILSMAN
#280

TEXAS
TART

by

Jon Sharpe

A SIGNET BOOK

SIGNET
Published by New American Library, a division of
Penguin Group (USA) Inc., 375 Hudson Street,
New York, New York 10014, USA
Penguin Group (Canada), 10 Alcorn Avenue, Toronto,
Ontario M4V 3B2, Canada (a division of Pearson Penguin Canada Inc.)
Penguin Books Ltd., 80 Strand, London WC2R 0RL, England
Penguin Ireland, 25 St. Stephen's Green, Dublin 2,
Ireland (a division of Penguin Books Ltd.)
Penguin Group (Australia), 250 Camberwell Road, Camberwell, Victoria 3124,
Australia (a division of Pearson Australia Group Pty. Ltd.)
Penguin Books India Pvt. Ltd., 11 Community Centre, Panchsheel Park,
New Delhi - 110 017, India
Penguin Group (NZ), Cnr Airborne and Rosedale Roads, Albany,
Auckland 1310, New Zealand (a division of Pearson New Zealand Ltd.)
Penguin Books (South Africa) (Pty.) Ltd., 24 Sturdee Avenue,
Rosebank, Johannesburg 2196, South Africa

Penguin Books Ltd., Registered Offices:
80 Strand, London WC2R 0RL, England

First published by Signet, an imprint of New American Library,
a division of Penguin Group (USA) Inc.

First Printing, February 2005
10 9 8 7 6 5 4 3 2 1

The first chapter of this book previously appeared in *Death Valley Vengeance,*
the two hundred seventy-ninth volume in this series.

 REGISTERED TRADEMARK—MARCA REGISTRADA

Printed in the United States of America

PUBLISHER'S NOTE
This is a work of fiction. Names, characters, places, and incidents either are the
product of the author's imagination or are used fictitiously, and any resemblance
to actual persons, living or dead, events, or locales is entirely coincidental.

The Trailsman

Beginnings . . . they bend the tree and they mark the man. Skye Fargo was born when he was eighteen. Terror was his midwife, vengeance his first cry. Killing spawned Skye Fargo, ruthless, cold-blooded murder. Out of the acrid smoke of gunpowder still hanging in the air, he rose, cried out a promise never forgotten.

The Trailsman they began to call him all across the West: searcher, scout, hunter, the man who could see where others only looked, his skills for hire but not his soul, the man who lived each day to the fullest, yet trailed each tomorrow. Skye Fargo, the Trailsman, the seeker who could take the wildness of a land and the wanting of a woman and make them his own.

Texas, 1861—
A stolen fortune, a prison where the guards are more
dangerous than the inmates, and a beautiful woman more
dangerous than both.

1

The man with the lake blue eyes sat his Ovaro stallion and stared down the slope at the campfire. A lone man squatted there, drinking coffee from a tin cup.

The time was near midnight on a lonely stretch of Texas prairie where, if you were lucky, you spotted a few adobe huts from time to time, and maybe a corral or two made of ocotillo canes. A man had to be hardy to live here. The local Indians were peaceful, but not the wandering war parties of the Apaches. They didn't like Mexicans any more than they liked whites.

The quarter moon helped hide the Trailsman and his Ovaro behind a copse of jack pines. The moon was pale and ragged gray rain clouds dragged across it. While this was the land where cattle was king, this section of the Rio Grande valley produced rich quantities of onions, spinach, carrots, and many fruits as well.

Skye Fargo was a man of experience. Take campfires—inviting as they always looked to a saddle-weary soul like Fargo—you could never be sure what you were getting into.

Fargo touched his holstered Colt, as if for luck, and kneed his horse down the grassy slope toward the fire. Hot coffee would taste mighty good on a chill April night.

Hearing Fargo approach, the campfire man stood up and peered into the darkness. "And who would that be?" he said, his right hand dropping to his own gun.

"Somebody who'd appreciate a little bit of fire and a cup of coffee."

"You mind puttin' your hands up when you come into the campsite here?"

Fargo laughed. "Been on this horse so long, I could use the exercise."

The man's caution was reassuring. He was as leery of Fargo as Fargo was of him.

Fargo, his face now painted with the red and gold of the campfire, eased himself into the small circle where the man had set his saddle, his saddlebags, and his rife. He held a Navy Colt.

"Sorry to be so suspicious," the man said.

He was tall, angular, with a sharply boned face and nervous dark eyes. He huddled deep inside his sheepskin.

Fargo climbed down from the stallion.

The man walked over and offered his hand. "Curtis Devol. Was a ranch hand till yesterday." He smiled. "Got a little too drunk in town the night before. Guess I told the boss what I thought of him. Guess it wasn't too pretty." He nodded to the fire. "Help yourself to the coffee. There're a couple biscuits left, too."

"Obliged. My name's Fargo, by the way. Skye Fargo."

Devol's eyes narrowed. "That name's familiar somehow." He shrugged. "Coffee's all yours, mister."

Fargo went back to his horse and dragged out his own tin cup. He haunched down to pick up the coffeepot. "So where you headed now?"

Devol stood above him on the other side of the fire. "Driftin', I guess. Don't have a skill or a trade. Wish I did. My brother's a blacksmith over to Santa Fe. Makes himself a right nice bit of money."

Devol wasn't kidding about lacking a skill—at least as an actor. The way his gaze suddenly flicked to the right, the way his jaws bulged in apprehension, the way his body gave an involuntary start—

Fargo didn't know what to expect for sure but he had a pretty good idea. He spun around on his haunches, hurled the coffeepot and its scalding contents up into the face of the man behind him, and then jerked to his feet, filling his hand with his Colt and blasting the revolver from Curtis Devol's gun hand.

The coffee-drenched man screamed and covered his face with his hands. Fargo stepped over to him and yanked the revolver from his hand, pitching it far into the shallow woods to the east. Fargo could see that the coffee had left the other man's face welted and violently scalded. Devol was favoring his hand.

"Take your friend down to the creek there," Fargo said to Devol. "Let him soak his face in the water for a while."

He walked back to his Ovaro and mounted. "I ever see either of you again, you're dead. You would've robbed me and killed me tonight and that ain't anything I'm likely to forget."

He rode back up the slope and disappeared into the night. He could hear the scalded man's sobs for a long time.

The town of Cross Peak was named because of the way two angled rock outcroppings looked like crossed swords when approached from the northeast. It was a shopping hub and railroad dispatch center for this part of Texas. The mayor, who had been an Easterner until six years ago, had decided to show these hicks how to build a civilized town. And damned if his intentions weren't impressive to look at.

Fargo couldn't recall ever seeing such a clean city. Three long blocks of stores, all kept freshly painted with board sidewalks running in the front and carefully raked streets dividing west side from east side. The people seemed friendlier here, too, as if the mayor had mandated that along with his orders about keeping everything clean and orderly.

The town was so friendly, in fact, that each of the four hotels had attractive young women standing at the entrances and beckoning Fargo to come over. He passed up the chance to meet the first three women but the fourth, a brunette in a yellow cotton dress that made her look downright festive, just couldn't be passed by.

He hauled his saddlebags up to the girl. "This town is so friendly, a fella could get suspicious."

She laughed, throwing her head back and revealing a long elegant neck. Bountiful breasts pressed against the yellow cotton. "Guess you haven't heard about the hotel war."

"What hotel war?"

"Right here. That's why the girls are standing out front. See if we can pick up business. There're just too many hotels for a town this size. Two of them have to go."

"Well, a pretty girl is a good way to get customers."

She leaned toward Fargo and said, "You ask for room sixteen. I'll be in there waiting."

"Is this part of the service?"

She winked. "Just every once in a while. When the spirit moves me, let's say."

Fargo checked into the hotel, asking for room sixteen. The desk clerk winked at him. Fargo was always annoyed by people who winked.

He found his room well-kept, with fresh sheets on the bed, a fresh flower in a narrow vase next to a washbasin uncorrupted by rust, and a selection of six magazines for his reading pleasure. There was a nice hooked rug on the floor and an even nicer rocking chair next to the window.

But nicest of all was the brunette waiting in bed for him. "I'll bet you're tired."

"I am. But I expect there are ways I can be revived."

"I expect there are, too. Get out of those clothes and we'll start with a nice back rub."

Voodoo, Fargo thought ten minutes later. There was no other explanation for the way her back rub relaxed and refreshed him. She sat completely naked on his buttocks as her fingers skillfully played across his back, her soft hirsute sex rubbing against him as she worked, leaning down sometimes so that she could press her full breasts against him. The hard nipples and the moisture of her sex made him almost crazy with need. At one point, she raised up, slid her hand down between his legs and took hold of his manhood. He couldn't ever remember desire this insane. He was dizzy, gasping as her fingers worked his lance as deftly as they had the muscles in his back.

When he couldn't stand it any more, he bucked up, took hold of her with one powerful arm, and angled her on the bed so that she was beneath him. His manhood was almost painfully huge by the time he stabbed into the hot juices of her mystery. She drove him even deeper by wrapping her legs around him and lifting herself to meet his every heated jab.

She reached ecstasy twice before he rolled off the bed, taking her with him, standing her up against the wall and then taking her from behind. Their frenzy was such that three different times he drove so deep and so hard that her

4

feet raised a few inches off the floor, her sumptuous body mounted on his thrusting rod.

But even now they weren't finished as she knelt before him, taking his epic spear in her mouth and bringing him to an even higher level of crazed frenzy.

Then there was just the blindness, the mindless roaring spasm of blood and sperm that the French called "the little death." The moment when there is only one reality, the release.

She lay in his arms for a time. "You haven't even asked my name."

"You haven't asked mine."

"I guess that's fair," she giggled.

"I sure hope you win the hotel wars."

"You think you might stay here again the next time you're passing through?"

"I'll make a point of it."

She reached down and touched his groin. "You've got quite a point yourself."

And then once again, they fell upon each other, ravenous as wolves.

It was dusk before she left. He slipped on his jeans and rolled himself a cigarette, smoking it as he stood at the window and looked out at the lamps being lit now that night was falling.

The one sight that marred the shiny new town was the small, gray, quarried-stone prison half a mile from Fargo's window. Cross Peak was a legendary hellhole. The murder rate was staggering. A lot of men were sent to Cross Peak knowing that they would never be seen or heard from again. The prison was a death sentence.

Fargo stripped down, washed off as much of the trail dust as possible, grabbed himself a magazine and lay down on the firm bed for a nap. He'd wake up around nine or so and then go buy himself a good meal.

He managed to read three pages of the magazine—the article concerned a United States senator's fears that buffalo were being overhunted and the Indians would soon lose one of their main sources of survival—when his eyes closed, the magazine tumbled to his chest, and he started to snore so loud the man in the adjacent room could hear him. His mouth still tasted of the nameless woman. It was a good, clean taste.

He fell asleep a happy man.

At first, Fargo assumed the sound was part of a dream he was having. But in the dream he was standing at a roulette wheel and winning more money than he'd ever accumulated in his life. So where did a gently sobbing woman come into a dream like that?

There was no woman in the dream.

But there was, he realized after rolling over on his side and opening one eye, a woman huddled in the corner of his room next to the bureau, and she was definitely making tiny kittenlike mewling sounds that could be confused with sobbing.

Yanking his Colt from the holster slung over the bedpost, Fargo sprang upward. "Who the hell are you?"

"You don't have any clothes on, mister. And I can see your thing."

2

"Am I always gonna look like this, Doc?" Branson said after Doc Myron Helms had jammed him into the examination chair and started looking over the burns.

Helms looked at Devol and winked. "Well, you weren't real pretty to begin with, so's I ain't sure it's gonna matter much."

Devol laughed. He was having a grand old time of it. Branson remembered the delight Devol took in the misery of others. Their two years together in Cross Peak prison, every time they'd hear about a con getting stabbed or shot or drowned by some other con, Devol would give out with this horse laugh that annoyed everybody in the prison. Devol was lucky he'd made it out alive.

"I don't want no sass, you old billy goat," said Branson, grabbing the doc by his goatee. "I want a straight answer."

"Well, there'll be some scarring I suppose, but I don't think it'll be much," the doc said and then slapped Branson's hand away. "I don't appreciate gettin' manhandled. I'm a doc. You're supposed to show respect."

"Only thing he ever respected," said Devol, "is money. He's a greedy bastard."

The office was in the parlor of Helms's home. An upright piano and a settee clashed with the odors of various medicines and the stench of numerous operations.

"I'll give you some ointment for it," Helms said. "Put it on twice a day."

"My face be all greasy?"

"For somebody as ugly as you are, you sure do worry a lot about your face." Helms could see that Branson was ready to reach for his beard again. "I keep a scalpel in my

7

hip pocket, son. I could cut your face up so bad no ointment would ever do you any good at all."

Branson said, "He's gonna pay."

"Who's gonna pay?"

"Fella they call the Trailsman."

"Heard he's a bad one. He the one done this to ya?"

"Yeah."

"Maybe next time he'll do you up permanent. I'd walk a
little wide if I was you, son." Helms winked at Devol again.

Devol gave that horse laugh of his.

The laugh brought all the prison years back. The painful
prison years. And the dream of a fortune Branson knew
would soon be his.

"No, please don't light the lamp," the woman said.

"Any special reason?" Fargo asked.

"Because they'll find me."

"Who'll find you?"

"The two men who've been chasing me. That's why I ran
into your room. They lost me for a while today but then
they found me again tonight."

"I'm going to pull my clothes on."

"I'll close my eyes. I appreciate you being a gentleman
and warning me."

He grabbed his clothes from the back of the rocking
chair. As he dressed, he asked questions.

"Why are they after you?"

"The gold mine."

"What gold mine?"

"The gold mine in Colorado. My daddy left me the map.
They used to be his partners. That's what they're trying
to get."

She was young, blond, and sweet, with a breathtaking
body packed inside a white chambray shirt, a pair of butter-
nuts, and cordovan riding boots. Her seeming innocence
only enhanced the allure of the body that inspired male
thoughts that were anything but innocent.

"Have you gone to the sheriff?"

"He wanted to see the map."

"You wouldn't show it to him?"

"You don't understand," she said. "I can't trust anybody.

I'm just a girl. I don't know who I can trust and who I can't. My name is Callie Bates, by the way."

"How do you know you can trust me, Callie?"

She hesitated and then said, "Don't take this personally but I don't trust you."

"So you just ran down the hall here and happened to duck inside my room?"

"Yes. Why?"

He sat down on the bed and rolled himself a cigarette. His features were stark and menacing in the lurid light of the lucifer. "Maybe I don't trust you—you ever think of that?"

"Why wouldn't you trust me? I'm just a girl. Helpless."

"With a face and body like yours, you're anything but helpless."

"So you don't believe me?"

"Right now, I'm not sure." He paused. "You hungry?"

"I hadn't thought about it. I guess not."

"I need a meal. A good one. Even if you don't."

She stood up and brushed her backside with hands quick and white in the shadowy room. "I don't want your meal and I don't want you. I'm not used to people accusing me of being a liar. Where I come from, a gentleman just naturally assumes a helpless girl is being honest."

He shrugged and walked out of his room.

When the counter woman set his plate in front of Fargo, his eyes widened with surprise and hunger. Now this was a real meal. A porterhouse steak, sliced potatoes, apple sauce, baked beans, and green beans. He was already on his third cup of coffee.

Since it was pushing ten, the Roundup Café was empty except for Fargo and a drummer reading at a table in the back of the place. Probably didn't want to face another lonely night in his hotel room, the drummer. Better to sit in the light with a few people around you than face the drummer's darkness.

Fargo thought about the girl. He could be grumpy when awakened, even if it was by a pretty girl. Maybe his grumpiness had overcome his good judgment. Why would she make up a story like that? What did she have to gain involving Fargo? And what was so strange about her ducking into Fargo's room? She had to duck in somewhere, didn't she? Maybe for once his suspicious nature had deceived him. Maybe she was, after all, the helpless young girl she insisted to be.

Still, he had doubts about her. The price you paid for surviving was skepticism. You had to hold back your belief, your trust. You didn't have to be cynical but you did have to be hard. In his time, he had been a cowboy, a gambler, a gunfighter, a rancher, a sheriff, a shotgun rider, and a wrangler, among many other temporary jobs. You believed people only after you'd been around them for a while and seen them in action.

He was brooding over all this when a sweet scent of perfume tantalized his nostrils. Before he had the chance to even look around, she sat next to him at the counter.

"I decided to forgive you," Callie Bates said.

"That's nice of you."

"I decided that my story probably does sound kind of suspicious."

He said, "You ate yet?"

"No. And now I'm really hungry." She glanced at the menu posted on a large sheet of paper on the wall facing the counter. Better than half the hand-printed words were misspelled.

"You know what I'm hungry for?"

"I didn't think people as scared as you're supposed to be got hungry."

She glared at him with those alarmingly seductive blue eyes. "Maybe I'll just get up and leave again. How would you like that?"

He shrugged. "Really wouldn't matter one way or the other."

She sulked. "Well, that's very nice."

But she didn't go anywhere and when the counter woman shuffled past, Callie Bates said, "Flapjacks, please, six of them." She glanced at Fargo and smiled. "My whole family's that way. Love flapjacks."

She told him the same story over again, except this time in more detail. She told it around a mouth stuffed with flapjacks. A delicate eater, she wasn't.

10

Maybe because he was familiar with the story now it sounded more believable. Life held a lot of strange twists and turns. Hers wasn't even all that unlikely. People did have legitimate gold maps that thieves tried to get their hands on. And thieves would be happy to prey on a young woman like Callie. She probably wasn't the innocent or naïf she pretended to be—one way a woman could always hook a man into helping her was to put on the helpless act—but now that he'd had time to think it through, he realized that she had nothing to gain by dragging him into her problems. She needed a friend who could help her get to that gold mine. He didn't plan to accompany her to Colorado but he couldn't see any harm in putting her safely on a train and getting her out of town.

She said, "Would you let me sleep on your floor tonight?"

"How about you sleep in the bed?"

Through a mouthful of flapjacks, she said, "I happen to be saving myself for my wedding night."

"I meant that I'd sleep on the floor."

She looked at him as if really seeing him for the first time. "Well, I'll be. Maybe you're a gentleman, after all."

He wasn't a gentleman, of course. What he was thinking was that if you put a man and a woman in a room with a bed in it, the two of them would most likely end up making love despite all previous protestations to the contrary. He'd just have to be patient. It might take a couple of hours but she'd invite him into bed at some point because she'd feel sorry for him. That was just how this sort of situation usually worked out.

"We close in ten minutes," the counter woman said, shuffling past again.

"I don't suppose there'd be time to griddle me up a couple more flapjacks," Callie Bates said plaintively.

Callie's little-girl tone obviously irritated the buxom woman. "I don't suppose there would be, dearie. Now finish up your coffee and get the heck out of here."

Fargo smiled. Callie had been gilding the lily—with her looks, she didn't need to act like a needy child, too—and this tough woman, who'd probably been on her feet for twelve hours, was right to mock her.

They finished up. They were the last customers of the

evening. Fargo paid their bill, and the two went out into a chilly night under a star-bright Texas sky. He had a sudden animal longing for warmth and shelter, safe from this night.

Callie Bates chattered as they walked slowly back to the hotel. Fargo didn't pay much attention. She was telling him about New York City and how that was going to be her very first stop when she sold the gold mine to some millionaire back east. He didn't give a damn about any of it. He wanted warmth and he wanted sex. His needs were apparently much simpler than those of Callie Bates.

There was an alley half a block from the hotel where they'd been hiding, waiting for Fargo and Callie to come along.

Fargo would have been able to draw down on them but just then Callie stubbed her booted toe against a loose board on the sidewalk and grabbed his gun arm for support.

There were two of them, both wearing bandanas over their faces. One of them wore a royal blue jacket with fancy yellow piping. They had their guns out and there wasn't a hell of a lot Fargo could do.

"It's them," Callie said. "I told you there were two of them after me."

What had seemed a lively, noisy street when they'd left the café ten minutes ago now seemed empty. Fargo could barely control himself from going for his gun. He wasn't worried about himself, but he didn't want to get Callie killed.

"We're taking the girl," the taller of the men said and grabbed for Callie's arm.

Fargo made his move, slamming himself into the man who'd reached for Callie, knocking aside his revolver. But the second man moved, too, bringing the barrel of his gun down hard across the side of Fargo's head, striking him twice before Fargo could even attempt to protect himself.

By then, it was too late. The cold darkness of a bottomless well awaited Fargo. The last thing he heard was Callie cursing her captors.

3

When the deputy threw a pan of water on him, Fargo came up swinging.

The sheriff, a man named William Clarke Plummer, said, "Damned drunks. Go fill up that pan again."

Fargo struggled to sit up. "You throw any more water on me, you sonofabitch, and I'll break every bone in your thick head." He rubbed at his face, damned irritated to be soaked this way by some hick punk who enjoyed his work a whole lot more than he should have.

The deputy, a scrawny kid who had more blackheads than he had brains, said, "He don't sound drunk, Sheriff."

"No, as a matter of fact, Erle, he don't."

"But he was sprawled all over the sidewalk. And facedown. And you know that's how most drunks get. They fall facedown and they don't move. It's like they're dead. In fact sometimes I can't tell if they're dead or alive when I try to wake them up."

Fargo, his holster and gun and boots gone, jerked to his feet, his head dripping water. "You ever think that somebody might've knocked me out?"

"Things like that don't happen very often in our little town, mister," the sheriff said, "and I don't appreciate you implyin' that they do. I run a tight ship here."

"Well, then your ship sprung a leak. I was walking back to my hotel and two men came up and stole a girl."

"Your girl?"

"I didn't say 'my girl' I said 'a girl.'"

"And what girl would that be?"

"She said she talked to you and you wouldn't believe her. Said her name was Callie Bates. A girl with a gold map."

"Aw, hell," Erle the deputy said. "She's crazy."

The sheriff, who was dressed in a dark suit that hid some of his middle-aged, jowly bulk, said, "I listened to her, mister. And I took her seriously enough that I had Erle here follow her. See if these two men she talked about actually existed. But they didn't. Or at least Erle never saw them, did you, Erle?"

"Nope." Erle wore a red-and-black-checkered shirt and jeans tucked into black cowboy boots. A faint fringe of hair on his upper lip indicated that he was trying to grow a mustache.

"Well, I don't care what Erle here saw or didn't see. I'm telling you that I saw them. And they kidnapped her."

"You put up a fight, did you?" Sheriff Plummer said.

"Pretty hard to fight when you're unconscious." He glared at Erle. "Get me a towel, kid, and make it fast."

Erle looked at the sheriff. The sheriff nodded.

Fargo took his first good look around. Four cells, two on one side of the small room, two on the other. Unlike most of the jails that Fargo had spent time in, this one was pretty clean. No smell of urine, puke, or blood. No dead animals flung into the room to make the conditions even slimier for the residents. No post where a man could be tied and lashed if he didn't cooperate with the man with the whip.

"She's a fine-looking young one, that's for sure."

"No argument there," Fargo said.

"A gal like that, she could make a man believe almost anything if she snuggled up to him enough."

"Well, there wasn't any snuggling. And I didn't say I believed her necessarily. But I saw the two men with my own eyes. And one of them knocked me out. And both of them took her away."

The deputy came back with the towel and tossed it to Fargo. He dried himself off and threw the towel back to Erle.

"I'll be leaving now," Fargo said.

"You will, huh?" the sheriff said. "I was under the impression that I made the decisions around here."

Fargo was tired of the cell and tired of these two. He made powerful fists and took a step toward the sheriff. "Just try and charge me with something, Sheriff. Go on. Just try it." His scowl was as insolent as he could make it.

The lawman had the good sense to take two steps back, out of range of Fargo's quick and deadly fists.

The deputy said, "You oughtn't to take that tone with Sheriff Plummer here. He's a mighty important man in this town."

"So what's it going to be?" Fargo said, taking a step closer to the lawman, animal-tight and ready to start slamming his fists into the man.

Plummer obviously did his best not to look afraid in front of his deputy. But a tic had developed under his right eye and he kept licking dry lips. His fear was obvious. But so was his resentment. He would concede this round to Fargo, but the fight was a long way from over.

"Let's go get Mr. Fargo his gun and boots, Erle," Plummer said mildly. "And then we'll say a prayer that he has the good sense to head straight out of town and never come within a hundred miles of it ever again."

He smiled at Fargo and followed his deputy to the front office.

The friendlier aspects of the town were waiting for Fargo less than half a block from the sheriff's office. Though Fargo was worried about Callie Bates, he did take the time to pause when a young woman of slender but unmistakable sensuality stepped down from the porch of the Excelsior Hotel and stopped right in front of him.

"You registered at a hotel?" she asked.

"Oh, I forgot. The hotel wars."

"You could really help me, mister."

"And how would that be?"

"Register here."

"I'm afraid I'm registered down the street."

"Oh."

The young woman wore a clingy dark silk dress, which full breasts defined on top and jutting hips defined in the middle. She had a wide face with a hint of Indian in the cheekbones and around the eyes. And a mouth made for love of the most exotic kind.

"Well, then I'll have to move out. I've haven't gotten any new guests today. And if I don't get at least three, I have to give up the room I get for free."

"I'm sorry."

He started to leave. She took his wrist. "Could you at least help me move my trunk? My room's on the ground floor. I'll have to find some other room for the night."

"Well, I've got other things to do. But I guess—"

"Good," she said, and pressed herself against him so that he could feel just how full and tempting her breasts were. She even managed to brush against his crotch. Then she turned and went up the steps of the Excelsior and inside.

Maybe he'd become jaded about hotels. They'd started to look the same, the kind he could afford anyway. Sure, you got the fancy ones in the big cities, but for the most part, hotels were pretty much like this one—and the one he was staying in—timber and stairs with carpeted runners.

She led him past a dozing desk clerk and down a narrow, sconce-lined hall. She inserted a key in room twelve and pushed her way inside.

By now, he was able to guess what she might be up to. But he decided to play it out. There were worse fates.

At least there was a trunk. That part of it was true. What they called a steamer trunk. He saw it as soon as she turned up the kerosene lamp.

"This it?"

She nodded. "It's pretty heavy."

And then she went into her act. She touched the back of her hand to her forehead and said, "Lord, I must've walked too fast or something. I feel like I'm going to faint."

And faint, she did. Or pretended to. She conveniently slumped backward onto the bed, the black silk dress pulling up high enough on her thigh so that he could see a hint of the sweet dark nest that lay between her slender thighs.

What the hell, he thought.

"Gosh, I sure hate to see a girl faint," he said.

He walked to the bed and leaned over her. She pulled him down with surprising force, taking his right hand and bringing it to the dark nest he'd glimpsed. She was warm and damp and luxurious already. And then the pure animal in him took over.

Less than a minute later, they were both naked and she was laying her legs on his shoulders and letting him sup of those large soft breasts of hers. The nipples were large too, large and chewy brown against the somewhat lighter shade of the aureoles. His tongue brought them to full stiffness

16

and his rod probed her as they inched toward a mutually satisfying motion.

She bucked whenever she reached satisfaction, and she reached satisfaction several times before he decided to let go. Slender as she was, there was great strength in the way she arched her back and took him all the way up inside her, clawing his back and buttocks as she did so.

Just before his own ultimate pleasure took place, she eased him out of her and slid down him so she could finish him with a tongue that was as wise and deft as any he'd ever encountered. She took him all the way between her lips, making tiny little moves with that tongue that only made his ultimate pleasure even more satisfying.

For five minutes, he just lay on his back and stared at the pressed-tin ceiling. Here was another one who knew what she was doing. These hotel wars were one damn bit of all right.

But he had things to do, and tempting as it was to press for another round of pleasure, he had to get up and get going.

He dressed.

"They really are going to kick me out," she said.

"Seriously?"

"Seriously."

She was as good at lying as she was at sex, making her difficult to read.

"How much is a room for one night?"

She told him.

"On my way out I'm going to sign in for a night."

Her reaction told him that she was telling the truth about getting kicked out. "Really? You'll do that?"

"I'll do that."

"I'm not a prostitute. I mean, I don't charge."

He smiled. "We've both got our reputations to consider here. You don't take money for sex and I don't pay money for sex. What I'm paying for is the room."

"Yes, indeed," she laughed. "The room."

On his way out to the street, he signed in for the night and paid the clerk the money he needed.

"Man waiting for you in your room," the plump, fancily mustached desk clerk said.

"You usually let people into other people's rooms?"

"This man said he was your brother."

"I don't have a brother."

The plump man had the grace to blush like a woman. "Oh, Lordy."

"What's he look like?"

The desk clerk described him. "Hey, where you going?"

"I'd tell you but if I did you'd probably tell him."

"I'm real sorry, Mr. Fargo."

Fargo took a deep breath. Probably wasn't a bad sort. Had just made a mistake was all. "I'll handle it from here. Don't worry about it."

"You won't tell my boss?"

"I said, 'Don't worry about it,' didn't I?"

"Thanks, Mr. Fargo. I appreciate it."

Fargo went around to the back of the two-story hotel. Cats played on piles of garbage. Ruby eyes burned deep into the heaps of refuse. Rats.

A fire escape built of two-by-fours led to the second floor and his room. He crept upward, Colt drawn and ready.

From various rooms he heard a cacophony of snoring, farting, coughing, sneezing, and even a little bit of praying.

The window of his room was opened an inch. The man inside would hear Fargo if he wasn't careful. No ballet dancer had ever moved more deftly on tiptoes than Fargo did right now. The difference was that few ballet dancers packed Colts.

He flattened himself against the exterior wall and then crouched down slowly so he could see inside the window.

The man had his back to Fargo. He sat in the rocking chair facing the door. A gun dangled from his hand.

From the description Fargo had gotten from the desk clerk, he knew that this was likely one of the men who'd taken the girl. He wondered what the hell was going on here. Why would they want to talk to him?

He got down on his haunches and quickly, before the kidnapper had time to react, pushed up the window and pointed the barrel of the Colt directly at the back of the kidnapper's head.

"I could cut your head in half with two bullets," Fargo said. "So if I was you, I'd set that gun on the floor and stand up real slow."

"Fargo?"

"You've got five seconds."

"Hell, man, don't do anything crazy."

The man set the revolver down and then stood up.

"Turn around now."

He was one of the men, all right. Fargo recognized the blue jacket with the fancy yellow piping.

Fargo pushed the window higher and crawled through. "Go over and sit in the corner."

"Why?"

"Because I said so."

The man shrugged and sat down in the corner. A gunless man stuffed into a corner presented no imminent danger.

Fargo turned up the lamp and sat down in the rocking chair. He hadn't realized till now who he was dealing with.

"The campfire last night. Devol."

"Yeah."

"So the other one was your saddle pard. What's his name?"

"Branson. And he hates you. Doc said his face won't heal for quite a while. That coffee you threw on him was mighty hot, mister."

"Where is he now?"

"With the girl."

"She alive?"

"Yeah."

"She hurt? You get the map from her?"

Devol snorted. "That map story. That's crap, mister. There ain't no map and there ain't no gold. But what there is is one hundred thousand in bank robbery money. And only one person knows where it is."

"The girl?"

Devol shook his head. "Her old man, Harold Bates."

"I'll be damned," Fargo said.

Devol smiled. "We all will, mister."

"Harold Bates," Fargo said and there was a hint of awe in his voice.

You could take every dime novel bank robber gang in the country and you still wouldn't reach the grand total of money Harold Bates had taken crisscrossing the land from Ohio to Wyoming and all the way down to the Mexican border. Eleven years his string had run. Even law-abiding

19

citizens paid him a grudging respect. It was like watching a great trapeze artist at work. How many death-defying tricks could he perform until fate or foolishness brought him down? But he got caught after the biggest payday of his life, one hundred thousand dollars. The posse had wounded his two accomplices and brought them in. They didn't catch Harold Bates for several days. He stood trial and was sentenced to life in prison. He had never killed anybody in the course of his robberies so the jury, which had taken a fancy to his reputation if not to the man himself, had spared him the gallows.

"He never told anybody where the money is," Devol said.

"You and Branson were with him that day?"

"Yeah."

"And now you want your cut."

"That's about the size of it."

Fargo whistled. He'd finally figured it out. Most of it, anyway. "So the girl makes up this story so I'll keep her safe from you grabbing her. If she'd told me her old man was Harold Bates, I might not have helped her."

Devol shrugged. "Yeah."

"And if I'm not mistaken, one of you goes to the prison and tells Bates that if he doesn't tell you where the money is, you'll kill his daughter."

Devol smiled. "I told Branson you were smart. Most people think gunnies aren't too bright."

"Two things wrong with that, pardner. I ain't a gunnie and a lot of gunnies are pretty damned smart, in fact."

"I guess you'd know more about that than I would, mister. But you got one thing wrong. Bates'd be so mad if we showed up to tell him about his daughter, he'd get us killed on the spot."

"He's in prison. How'd he get you killed?"

"He's a big man there. He had some other money stashed away, too. We served our time in the same prison Bates is in. He paid off the head guard. Bastard named Rafferty. Rafferty'll do anything he asks except break him out because if he done that, he'd be wearing prison stripes himself."

All Fargo said was, "Me."

"That's it exactly, Fargo. You want to see that girl alive again, you better do just what me'n Branson tell you. You go to the prison and tell Bates we want to know where the money is or else." Devol smiled. "I'd say that's a right smart plan, wouldn't you? He'll be impressed that somebody like the Trailsman is in on everything. He'll know better than to try and stall us. You just wait and see."

"So I go to the prison and get him to tell me where the money is," Fargo said, "and then I tell you."

"That's about right," Devol said.

"And then you kill me and the girl and keep all the money for yourself."

Devol laughed. "You're a big boy, Fargo. You can take care of yourself. Otherwise—"

"Otherwise, the girl dies."

"That's about the size of it. Of course, she don't die till I've had my fun with her. I imagine Branson's havin' some fun with her right now."

Devol obviously loved the villain role. Made him feel powerful. Fargo had seen it in all kinds of men, from bank robbers and rapists to killers. Bad enough they did their deeds, they had to strut around afterward bragging on it— the influence of dime novels and theater plays. If you were gonna be bad, you might as well be real bad.

"I guess I don't have much choice."

"I guess you don't. But I've got a warning for ya."

"Yeah," Fargo said. "You told me. Branson."

"You should see his face."

Fargo moved swiftly. The way Devol sat against the wall, his legs parted slightly, left a clear opening for Fargo's boot. He caught Devol clean in the balls.

Devol screamed.

"I'd be just as happy if I never saw either of your faces again," Fargo snapped.

Then he reached down, yanked the punk to his feet, dragged him to the door, and pitched him out into the hallway.

A fat drunk in a top hat and expensive suit was attempting to negotiate his way to his room. Without looking down, he stepped over the writhing form of Devol on the corridor floor. He also tipped his hat in Fargo's direction and said, "Good evening, sir."

"Good evening to you, sir," Fargo said, and slammed shut his door.

* * *

Harold Bates had never gone the queer route, though God knew he could understand the loneliness that drove some men to it.

He was able to bribe the head guard Rafferty to bring him just about anything he wanted in prison. Except for two things—a woman and freedom.

Bold as Rafferty was in his cruelty and corruption, even he wouldn't try to sneak a female into the prison. If the men got so much as a glimpse of her, there would be a riot that would likely reduce this prison to ruin and rubble, and then he would pay. Everybody in the prison knew that Warden Grieves had killed more than his share of prisoners. He wouldn't hesitate to kill Rafferty. And Rafferty knew it. Otherwise, his guard protector was reliable. Not even the angriest, craziest inmates trifled with Nick Rafferty. Rafferty had, variously, stabbed, drowned, beaten, and torched inmates during his seven-year tenure.

The worst time for Harold Bates was this time of night when his insomnia was at its worst. He had, unlike most inmates, his own cell. He had plenty of tobacco, a quart of bourbon, many current magazines and newspapers, a variety of foods, and a bed with a regular store-bought mattress and blanket. If the other inmates resented this—and they did, of course—they wouldn't say anything directly to Bates about it. Not when Bates's protector was Nick Rafferty.

He yawned. He scratched. He daydreamed. And it was the money daydream. A hundred thousand dollars in bank loot. Imagine the female flesh that could buy. He didn't want romantic love. He wanted sex, and sex with women of all kinds—all shapes, ages, colors. He wanted to frolic in their flesh and juices like a kid in a swimming hole on a hot Texas afternoon, and he had enough money stashed to do it.

He had thought of escaping before. Rafferty was the only one who could make it possible and he'd want a lot of money up front to pull it off. That could be taken care of. The real problem was what happened after he got away from the prison. With his arthritis and fading vision, he wasn't a youngster. And once he got away, Nick Rafferty would no longer be able to help him. He'd be on his own. This area of Texas was crowded with lawmen eager to make a rep for themselves. They were just as crooked, most

22

of them, as the men they pursued, but as long as they could hang a badge on their shirts, they could get away with damned near anything—including shooting Harold Bates after forcing him to tell where he'd hidden the bank loot. They'd end up with the money, not the bank.

But in spite of all the dangers of escape, he knew he couldn't deal with prison life much longer. If the men didn't come here as rapacious animals, they soon became such. That was the price of surviving. Harold Bates was a bank robber who used violence only when absolutely necessary. These men used violence to ease their frustrations, to establish dominance, to amuse and impress other inmates.

Harold Bates didn't belong here. And he knew that, risky or not, he'd soon have to make his break.

4

The prison walls were quarried stone. The three guard towers glinted in the sun. A Mexican in an awfully snappy khaki uniform stood at a door built into the massive front gate, a double-barreled shotgun hanging from his right hand. His mouth broke into a sneer until Fargo got close. The sneer disappeared. The Mexican had apparently decided that Fargo was not the sort of man one sneered at.

"I need to see the warden."

"There are many such requests, my friend. But few are granted."

"I need to see him."

They stared at each other, the Mexican's glare holding steady for maybe thirty seconds. Then he looked away and sighed. He turned back to the door where he opened a slot about three quarters of the way up. He shouted into the slot, "Rafferty, come here."

The Mexican slammed the slot shut and turned back to Fargo. "You want to see the warden for what reason?"

"For reasons that are none of your business."

"If you don't tell me, you will have to tell Rafferty." He smiled. Apparently his balls had dropped back down again. "And Rafferty is much harder to work with than I am."

Baking sun, ninety-three degrees, and not quite eight thirty in the morning. And not much sleep last night—this sonofabitch was pushing his luck. The mood Fargo was in, he'd pound on both the guard here and Rafferty at the same time.

Rafferty was a tall bald man with a fleshy face and cunning blue eyes. He didn't look the least impressed with Fargo. "Sanchez, you think I ain't got nothin' better to do than carry messages? We got to dig some fresh latrines before it hits a hundred. I don't want no men keelin' over the way they did yesterday. That stupid-ass woman from the prison board is supposed to show up here sometime today. She sees men passin' out, she'll write it up and then the warden'll gnaw on my ass for a month."

Sanchez nodded to Fargo. "He wants to see the warden."

"How come he wants to see the warden?"

"He will not say." Sanchez smiled. "He is one of the huffy ones."

"Huffy, huh?" Rafferty said. "Then tell him to kiss your ass and get back on his horse."

Sanchez looked at Fargo. "You see what I say, amigo? Rafferty is much tougher to deal with than I am."

The sweep and the power of the right hook surprised even Fargo—he reasoned that he must have been a hell of a lot angrier than he'd realized. The punch came up under Rafferty's jaw and lifted him a good foot off the desert sand. The damage didn't end there. Rafferty slammed into the wall, smacking his head hard against the stone.

He was tough, though. Even given the punch Fargo had landed, even with slamming his head against stone, Rafferty sprang off the wall and jumped at Fargo with no thought of protecting himself. He didn't give a damn about being hurt. He just wanted vengeance.

Fargo was able to duck the first few punches. He managed to get off a good body shot, a severe punch to Rafferty's rib cage.

Then the accuracy of Rafferty's punches improved and Fargo found himself on the wrong end of three howling fists that blacked him out for a couple of long, spooky moments.

The fight proceeded, the two men both good, quick fighters. Rafferty was the first to get a bloody nose, Fargo the first to get a large bruise above his eye. They circled, ducked, lunged, threw the best punches they could, and then went back to the safety of circling. They were throwing so many punches so hard that both were tiring badly. They didn't care about the beauty or grace of their pugilistic skills—they just wanted to hurt the hell out of each other.

"A buggy!" Sanchez warned. "Maybe the woman from the prison board."

If either of the fighters heard Sanchez, they paid him no heed. They kept on pounding away on each other.

"The buggy!" Sanchez warned again, much more urgently this time.

The fight was going to end without really being finished unless Fargo acted quickly. He bobbed to the right and smashed a stone hand hard against Rafferty's right temple. Without pause, he stabbed a left hand hard into Rafferty's sternum. Then he went to the right temple again.

Rafferty looked like a man whose nervous system had shut down. His eyes were wild but didn't seem to see; his legs shook and trembled but didn't seem to take him anywhere; and his arms windmilled to keep him from falling over backward but to no avail. He was going down and no doubt about it.

Fargo grabbed the descending man and snapped, "Open the door, Sanchez, before the prison lady gets here! I'll hide Rafferty inside!"

Sanchez ran on pure instinct now. He could lose his job if he permitted the prison woman to know of this fight. He could hear her now: What kind of prison assaults visitors who come to see the inmates? The warden would fire him for sure and then Sanchez would be forced to return to backbreaking seasonal farm work. His wife warned him that this prison guard job was a dangerous one, but he'd said to her that he would rather face crazed prisoners every day than do stoop labor. He was too old and too proud for stoop labor.

Sanchez opened the door quickly. Fargo got his arm around Rafferty's waist and hauled him inside the prison.

Three dormitorylike buildings took up most of the interior. There was a fourth building that appeared to have a workshop on the bottom and offices on the top. Many of the prisoners would be working the fields during the day. Gray uniformed inmates were everywhere, scrubbing down wagons, making barrels, sawing lumber, painting buildings faded by the sun. Fargo didn't see any conversations going on. The large number of khaki-clothed guards did a good job of intimidating the inmates, making sure that nobody was having a good time.

Rafferty had already vanished.

Fargo went up to a guard. "Place I can clean up a little?"

The guard smiled coldly. "Rafferty?"

"Yeah."

"He's a mean bastard."

"Yeah, but I was a little meaner."

"See that door over there?"

Fargo nodded.

"You can wash up in there. You here to see the warden?"

"Yes, and I'd be obliged if you'd take me to his office."

"You know what you should've done with Rafferty, don't ya?"

"What?"

"Slipped him some money. Rafferty. Most of the time, that's all he wants." The smile got wider. "Of course, there are some people he just don't take a shine to."

Five minutes later, after washing, taking his shirt out and brushing the sand and dirt off, Fargo looked a lot better. He had the bruise above his eye but even that didn't look so bad when Fargo got cleaned up and got his hair combed again.

In the reception area of the warden's office, an inmate sat rubber-stamping receipts of some kind. Not even after the guard said, "Dooley, man here to see the warden," did the inmate stop what he was doing and look up. He worked continuously until he finished the stack he was working on.

By this time, the guard had left. The inmate raised his head and took his account of Fargo. "You have an appointment?"

"No."

"Most folks get an appointment before they come here."

"I didn't know that."

"He's pretty busy."

"Everybody's pretty busy. Including me."

The sharpness of Fargo's tone made the inmate narrow his eyes. "You better be nice to me, mister. Otherwise you won't get to see him even with an appointment."

"Is that right?" He was faster than the inmate. He moved around the desk to the pebbled-glass door marked WARDEN in seconds. He opened the door and walked in.

Warren G. Grieves was not a man made for city suits. He was thick, squat, bald, and had a face as flat, battered, and ferocious as that of an ancient warrior. His gray suit and white shirt failed to give him the air of a civilized man he hoped it would. He kept a Navy Colt on his desk and the instant the door burst open, he grabbed it and pointed it directly at Fargo. "You'd better have one hell of a good story, mister, otherwise you're going to be very sorry you did this."

The inmate bolted through the door and said, "Warden, this man don't have no appointment. And he just come in here on his ownsome."

Grieves said, "Get out of here, Jimmy. Go see one of your boyfriends."

Jimmy blushed and withdrew, closing the door quietly.

Grieves surveyed Fargo's face and said, "If I didn't know better, I'd say you'd just met up with our Mr. Rafferty. But I've got him out digging latrines this morning."

"He was near the gate. Sanchez called him over."

"How much you pay him to get in?" Grieves's laugh surprised Fargo.

"I guess that was my mistake. That and swinging on him."

The amusement remained on the warden's wide flat face. "You picked a bad one to swing on."

"Well, I got the better of him by a punch or two."

"Is that a fact?" Grieves wasn't being ironic. His amusement changed to a quiet, serious interest in the man who stood in front of him. "You really got the better of him?"

"It wasn't that impressive. Could easily have gone the other way. He's a tough one."

"Yes, but to beat him at all—" He set the gun down on his desk. "Have a seat. What's your name?"

"Fargo."

"Fargo?" Now it was the warden's turn to be surprised. "Skye Fargo? The Trailsman?"

Fargo shrugged. "Guess so." He was embarrassed sometimes by his reputation, considering it overblown. He was a hard man who did what a hard man did when the situation required it, but he wasn't the mythic figure that men liked to talk about over beers in saloons. Nobody could live up to that kind of reputation. And Fargo didn't even try.

"Your ears'll be burning tonight, Mr. Fargo."

"And how'll that be?"

"Poker night. I'll have to tell all the boys that I met you today." He laughed again. "Rafferty know who you are?"

"I don't think so."

"Wait till I tell him. Maybe he won't feel so bad about getting whipped."

Fargo was going to object to the word "whipped"—he hadn't "whipped" Rafferty, he'd just outpunched him a few times—but he decided to get down to business.

"I came here to visit somebody," Fargo said.

"Oh? And who might that be, Mr. Fargo?"

"Harold Bates."

This was the heartiest laugh of all. Grieves sat back in his tall leather chair and said, "So you're after that hundred thousand dollars, too."

Harold Bates said, "What the hell happened to you?"

"Some sonofabitch jumped me from behind," Rafferty told him.

"Some inmate?"

"Nah. Some visitor."

"Visitor? Since when do visitors jump guards?"

"Had some wild hair up his ass is all I know. But I fixed him pretty good."

"Looks like he didn't do too bad on you, though," Bates said, noting the black eye and the nostrils that were rimmed with dried blood.

Rafferty glowered at him. Bates didn't care. In fact, he made a point of irritating the big guard every once in a while. It reminded Rafferty of who was in control of their relationship. Rafferty had built a nice life for himself on the money he got for protecting Bates. He wasn't about to make any move on his money man.

They were in the barn. Bates had learned to shoe horses in here. He served as apprentice to a real blacksmith named Dutch Prentiss who had used his anvil and hammer to crush the skull of the man who'd slept with his wife. He bragged that he'd pounded half the man's skull completely flat. Bates figured Dutch was so crazy he'd do the same thing to an inmate someday, and was careful never to make him mad. Dutch scared the hell out of him.

"I want out of here."

Rafferty had been cleaning himself up with warm water from a basin. He wiped his face on his khaki sleeve. "Yeah, and I wanna be King of England, too."

"I'm serious."

"I thought we discussed this a long time ago."

"We did. But I've changed my mind."

"I can't do it. They'd know I helped you and then they'd throw me in here myself. Wouldn't the boys love that, gettin' their hands on me."

Bates laughed. "That crazy bastard Dutch'd probably put your head on that anvil over there and start poundin' away."

"That ain't funny."

"One way or the other, I'm gettin' out of here. And right away."

Rafferty spat in the dirt of the barn floor. "Not with my help, you ain't."

He strode out into the sunlight and never once looked back.

"You say you're a cousin of Mr. Bates?" Warden Warren G. Grieves said.

"That's right. Second cousin. But we were raised on the same farm."

"He's old enough to be your father."

"He was my father. The way he looked out for me, I mean. Nobody ever bothered me when Hank was around."

"You called him 'Hank?' "

"Uh-huh."

"We call him 'Harold.' "

Fargo nodded. "That's his grown-up name, I guess."

"So this doesn't have anything to do with that bank loot he's got hidden somewhere?"

"I just thought I'd pay a visit on poor old Hank."

" 'Hank,' eh?" Grieves smiled again. "I've always heard how good you were with a gun and your fists. But nobody warned me how good you were slinging the bullshit. 'Poor old Hank.' " He laughed. "I'll have to tell that one to the boys, too."

If a girl's life hadn't been at stake, Fargo would have been forced to laugh, too. His whole story about "cousin Hank" was transparent as hell.

"Well, I'm sorry you had that dustup at the gate, Mr. Fargo."

He was about to say more when someone rippled three knuckles across the glass of his office door.

"Yes. Who is it?"

"Rafferty," said the voice from the other side of the pebbled glass.

"Well, think of that, Mr. Fargo. I may get to see one hell of a good boxing match right in my office here."

For a guy who looked as if he should be toting a shield and a spear, Fargo thought, this warden sure did like to laugh a lot.

"Come right in, Rafferty," Grieves announced grandly. "There's an old friend of yours here just waiting to see you again."

Three minutes earlier, when Rafferty had first come into the warden's outer office, Jimmy McFee said, "Hey, what happened to you?"

"Some cowboy jumped me from behind."

"I bet I know who you're talkin' about."

"Who?"

"Man named Fargo. You ever heard of the Trailsman?"

"Heard of him, I guess. Why?"

"Fargo and the Trailsman are one and the same." He nodded to the warden's door. "Fact is, he's in there right now."

Rafferty glared at the door. It wasn't even ten o'clock and the day was already a bastard. Rafferty's pregnant wife wouldn't have sex with him to start off with. Then he got kicked around by this Fargo, and then his main source of income, Harold Bates, threatened to jeopardize their whole setup by making the one demand Rafferty couldn't meet. . . .

The big problem was Bates. If he didn't help the outlaw escape, Bates could always threaten to tell the warden all about the money and all the things that Rafferty did for that money. But if he did help Bates escape, it wouldn't be long before Rafferty would be blamed. A lot of the men here knew all about Bates and Rafferty. You couldn't keep a thing like that private in a prison. He was the only con who got good drinking whiskey, expensive cigars, excellent food, and a private cell. And everybody knew who got them for him.

The third option was to kill Bates. Rafferty had killed before and would kill again. He didn't take any special joy in killing the way some men did. It was just a matter of people getting in his way. If you got in his way and stayed there long enough, he'd think on it a while and then kill you. The thinking on it wasn't about if he should kill you or not. The thinking on it was about how to do it without getting blamed for it. That caliber of thinking took a little while.

"What's he talking to the warden about?" Rafferty snapped.

"Bates."

"Bates?" A chill came over Rafferty. He could feel goose bumps on his arms. Bates? Now why the hell would a man like Fargo want to talk to a man like Bates? Something was going on here and Rafferty didn't like it at all. You got signs, portents sometimes. You would hear something and even though nothing specific was said you heard an ominous turn of events coming your way. Once in New Orleans, Rafferty had drunkenly taken a whore as a lark to a fortune teller, and damned if a couple of things the scurvy old lady had predicted didn't come true a few months later. Ever since then he'd believed in a shadowy world that most people feared to see or even acknowledge.

Rafferty started for the pebbled door.

"Wouldn't do that if I was you. The warden can see your shadow on the glass. That's how he caught me listening one morning."

"I need to find out what's goin' on in there."

Jimmy McFee grinned. "You're curious about a man like this here Fargo talkin' to a man like Bates, ain't ya? And I don't blame ya. Maybe he's after that hundred thousand Bates got hid away."

Everybody in the prison knew about that money. It had grown into myth. Rafferty was the only reason that somebody hadn't beaten the information out of Bates. Anybody stupid enough to go up against Rafferty would be real dead real soon and everybody in here knew it.

But a man like Fargo . . . after this morning, no way was Fargo worried about Rafferty, that was for sure.

Rafferty's mind roiled with different ideas about what Fargo was doing here. The one thing all the ideas had in common was the hundred thousand dollars.

"You get me some good whiskey, Rafferty. I'll see what I can find out for you."

"A pint."

"Two pints."

"Two pints? I don't have that kinda money."

"You don't but Bates does. Just tap him for a little more the way you always do. He'll come through for ya. And then you can come through for me."

"The hell with you," Rafferty said and strode to the warden's door.

Thirty seconds later, he was inside the office.

"I believe you've met Mr. Fargo here, Mr. Rafferty," the warden said, jovial and stupid as ever.

"Horses, horses, horses," Dutch Prentiss said. "That's all I ever get."

Harold Bates sighed. A couple of times a week Dutch gave one of his two speeches as the two men banged and clanged away on their anvils or stooped and banged away on the horses they were shoeing. As Dutch's assistant Bates had had to learn a whole new language such as braze and smithy and Damascus steel. He also had to learn all about the strange and frightening and unstable world of Dutch Prentiss.

The first Prentiss speech was actually pretty short. It was really just a litany of names of all the people Dutch wanted to kill within these prison walls. Depending on his mood, some weeks he'd only kill half the men in here—that he'd kill the warden and all the guards went without saying—and other weeks he might be so worked up he'd talk about killing damned near everybody, including the horses. If he was really worked up, he'd include a variety of killing methods in his bloody monologue.

Bates had learned how to turn off his hearing when the list of names started pouring out of Dutch's mouth.

The second speech had the virtue of at least being interesting, at least the first three hundred times Bates had heard it.

"I am an artist, Harold," Dutch would always begin, the

slabs of his muscles glistening with sweat, his stark, crazed brown eyes lifted heavenward even as he slammed away at a shoe on his anvil. Dutch did a lot of reading in here and had developed a flowery way of talking when he gave his little speeches. In the mock-eloquent way he spoke you could hear the madness that had led him to flatten the skull of the man who'd bedded his wife. He'd been spared the gallows only because his uncle was a good friend of the governor.

"I am an artist, Harold. I shouldn't be making shoes for these stupid smelly animals. Do you know what I should be doing as an artist, Harold? I should be like the blacksmiths who served the kings of Europe. Do you know what those blacksmiths created, Harold? They created rapiers and swords and stilettos. Weapons of war, Harold. The finest weapons that could be found anywhere. Do you know that kings would kidnap blacksmiths from other kings? That's how important these men were. They didn't shoe these stupid smelly animals, Harold. And that is what's in my heart, Harold. The need to be an artist. The need to create something so that the world will know that I mattered to my time here on earth."

And then he would stand still for long moments, tears streaming down his broad cheeks, and he would say, "Someday, Harold, my art will be known throughout the world."

This morning, as usual, Bates had no idea what to say. He muttered, "That's true, my friend. Someday the whole world will understand."

He spoke slowly, watching Dutch's eyes carefully for how each word affected Dutch. If the madman's eyes started to narrow—

"You understand about art, Harold. I sensed that in you the moment they brought you in here."

"Well." Bates smiled, almost shyly. "My art's a little different from yours, Dutch. My art is, I rob banks."

"Art is art!" Dutch thundered.

"Well, that's true, I guess."

"Of course it's true. I'm an artist. You're an artist. We should hold ourselves in greater esteem than these lowlifes we have to live with."

"You've sure got a point there, Dutch. Yes, indeed, you sure do."

All the while hoping that Dutch didn't take offense somehow and hurl his mighty hammer at Bates's head.

Bates never argued with Dutch because he did not want to give Dutch any reason to put his, Harold's, head on the anvil. Also, it was Dutch's niece who always snuck money into the prison for Harold. This was the money he'd deposited under an assumed name in the Cross Peak bank, not the hundred thousand he'd hidden elsewhere. The nice thing about niece Nina was that she worked here in the prison, as about twenty other locals did. She oversaw the kitchens and did all the ordering from town. Whenever Bates needed money, he told Dutch, who in turn told Nina. Bates paid Nina ten percent of whatever he asked her to withdraw. She'd done well for herself.

After Dutch settled down from his insane opera about art and fame, Bates asked, "Think you could see Nina today?"

"You spend a lot of money, my friend."

"Yes, I do. And this time I'm going to spend more than ever. And the thing is, I'm going to need it yet today. Think she can handle that?"

"She'll certainly try. She is a good girl."

"Yes, she is. She certainly is."

Bates had always been an impetuous man. When he made his mind up to do something, he damn well wanted to do it now. His plan to escape was no different. He wanted to get out of here. Once he'd recognized the emotional need to escape, once he'd raised the subject with Rafferty, he was as good as gone. He was going to make it impossible for Rafferty to turn him down.

"You know what I do sometimes, Harold?" Dutch said, interrupting Harold's thoughts.

"No, Dutch, what do you do sometimes?"

"You see this horseshoe I'm working on?"

"Yep. That's a horseshoe, all right."

"Not in my mind it isn't. In my mind it is a piece of metal that will become the finest dirk stiletto ever made." He paused and looked down at the fire-tipped horseshoe he was pounding. "This is the only way—by pretending, I mean—that I can keep my sanity."

Bates almost laughed, which would have been a stupid and dangerous thing to do. Sanity? Crazy Dutch Prentiss probably hadn't been sane one full day in his life.

"Yes, I can see that it's a struggle to keep your sanity in a place like this. I have to struggle with it myself sometimes."

"That's because you're an artist, Harold. An artist!"

"Listen, Dutch, not to change the subject, but how soon do you think you could sneak off and talk to Nina?"

Both Fargo and Rafferty had good reason to pretend their feud was over. Fargo wanted to see Harold Bates and Rafferty wanted to keep his job. They shook hands as the warden insisted and then Rafferty, as Grieves instructed, took Fargo over to the west end of the prison where a large room decked out in tables and chairs was set up for visitors. Prisoners came from a door at the far side of the room, directly down a corridor that was part of a cell block.

On regular visiting days this room would be noisy with mothers bringing children in to see their fathers. The little ones would be running around, not realizing where they were or what it meant. The older ones would be bored, gaping around. The mothers and fathers would frequently be in tears together. There was a lot of quiet pain in this room on visiting days, regret and remorse and dreams dashed forever.

Neither Fargo nor Rafferty had spoken once on their walk over. Both were ready to start punching again. Fargo just didn't like the bastard. There was something about a man who made his living keeping men in cages—a necessity at times, of course, but it still wasn't a noble calling.

Rafferty pointed to a table and chair. "Sit there. I'll get Bates." He started to walk away then stopped and turned back to Fargo. "This ain't over, cowboy."

"I was kinda hopin' you'd say that."

"I'm gonna find you sometime and make you regret you ever met me."

Fargo smiled and looked around the room. "I'd be happy to go again right now."

"Sure you would, and get my ass fired. You'd like that a lot."

Rafferty left, disappearing into the barred door that led into the guts of the prison. Fargo didn't enjoy the wait.

There was nothing he liked about prison. He had a vague fear that he'd end up in a cell himself by mistake or fluke.

Harold Bates was a small, robust man who walked with more of a strut than you expected to see from an imprisoned man. He was talking to Rafferty when the barred door was opened and they walked into the visitors' room. Fargo noted that their relationship seemed pretty casual for a guard and a prisoner. They seemed to be talking as equals. For a moment, it even seemed as if Bates might be giving Rafferty hell about something.

Fargo tucked the information away. Something was going on here that might be useful later on.

Bates walked the last ten feet to Fargo's table alone. He was still strutting. He'd been known to be something of a dandy in his bank robbing days.

He came over and sat down. Fargo started to introduce himself but Bates glared across the room at Rafferty and said, "I thought you were going to step outside and roll yourself a smoke."

Rafferty scowled and then walked insolently out the nearest door.

"You kind of run this place, do you?" Fargo asked.

Bates smiled. "Kind of, I guess you'd say."

"Never saw a guard take orders from a con before."

"Life is just full of surprises," Bates said merrily. "That's the biggest reason I don't want to die. Afraid I'll miss out on one of those surprises, I guess." Then, leaning toward Fargo, he said, his voice angry now, "Rafferty told me who you are, Fargo. But don't think I'm going to cut you in because I'm afraid of your reputation. I don't give a damn how many men you've killed or how many men you've helped send to prison. You're not going to get any part of that hundred thousand. Nobody is. It's mine. And I intend to keep it that way."

"Sounds like you've got it all figured out."

Bates was still angry. "You know how many tinhorn sonsabitches have come here to try and get me to tell them where that money is? They call themselves reporters but I know what they are and what they're after. And not one of them got so much as one tiny clue from me. And you're not going to, either."

"I hate to spoil your little spiel about what a crafty old coot you are, Bates, but I'm not here for myself. I'm here because two saddle bums named Devol and Branson forced me to come here."

"Devol and Branson? And you say you're not after the money? That's all they care about. They say I took the money for myself. And that's true. But what they probably didn't mention is that I overheard 'em plotting to kill me as soon as the robbery was over. They didn't think they needed me anymore. And since I knew so much about 'em, they didn't want to take the chance that I might turn 'em over to he law." He was angry again. "That money belongs to me, Fargo, and nobody else. I don't share my money with double-crossers, that's for sure."

"There's something else you should know," Fargo said.

For the first time, Bates looked as if he couldn't anticipate what Fargo was going to say. "Yeah, and what would that be?"

"They kidnapped your daughter."

"Callie?"

A grin like that of a five-year-old appeared on Bates's face. "Aw, hell."

Fargo wondered what kind of man would grin when told that his daughter had been kidnapped.

The grin became a belly-bouncing laugh. "So they told you to come out here and get me to tell you where the money is or they'd kill Callie? Is that it?"

"That's it," Fargo said.

Bates had actual tears in his eyes—from giggling so hard. "Well, you tell them to go right ahead and shoot her. And with my blessing. I wouldn't raise a finger to help that little bitch. She was plotting right along with them to kill me."

5

Fat bitch was lying down again. Goddamn cabin they lived in hadn't been clean in weeks. No supper ready. Bitch.

Rafferty had stopped off for a few beers at a saloon on his way back from the prison. He'd hoped the beers would relax him but they'd had the opposite effect. They'd only incensed him all the more. He was still hurting, physically and mentally, from the beating he'd taken from Fargo, and he was still angry that Harold Bates had brought up the escape thing again. If he helped the con escape, it would all come tumbling down. And fast.

Rafferty made as much noise as possible heating up some coffee and fixing up a large slice of bread with some near-rancid butter. She couldn't even keep fresh butter on hand for him. If he complained, all he'd get was her litany of woman's woes about having a kid.

He didn't want a kid and he didn't want her. In fact, where she was concerned, he couldn't even look at her anymore. Gone was the thin, pretty girl he'd married, replaced by her fat, ugly cousin. Or so it seemed to Rafferty—some sort of joke pulled on him. Where was the little gal he'd married? So sweet and obedient? Who was this cow masquerading as his wife?

When he finished his sullen meal, he grabbed a pint of rotgut and went outside to watch dusk settle in. The sky was a color of pink only a dusk sky can ever be. The stars were out but only with a certain reluctance, it seemed. Usually there were more out by now. There was a slight wind, and it was cooler tonight. A lot better than the heat of the day, maybe even a little uncomfortable.

In the old days, he could slide into bed with his old lady, that sweet, pretty, obedient little woman . . .

For the next half hour, Rafferty sat on a tree stump in his front yard and took stock of his life. Some life. He was only twenty-seven and felt ninety sometimes. The baldness didn't help. He didn't even daydream about better circumstances anymore. What was the point of daydreaming about things that would never be? He was sick of dreams, sick of his job, sick of the woman who'd become a slovenly cow. In that regard, he was like Harold Bates. He wanted to escape.

A female voice behind him said: "You get yourself some supper, Nicholas?"

Nicholas. He hated that name. Nicholas. It was her little term of endearment but it had long ago lost its ability to endear.

"Yeah," he said, without turning around to look at her. Who'd want to look at a cow like her, anyway? "I had a steak and sliced potatoes and apple sauce and pie. They were all on the counter waitin' for me when I got home."

"No need for sarcasm, Nicholas. I can't help it if I can't get nothin' done. In case you hadn't noticed, I'm pregnant."

"Hell, you were just as lazy before you were pregnant." He was getting mean. He didn't give a damn.

"That's not a very nice thing to say to the woman that's gonna have your baby."

Baby. They'd been trying to have a baby the entire ten years of their marriage. Just about the time Rafferty started thinking of walking away from it all, she ups and gets pregnant. He sure didn't want a baby, and didn't want her, either.

"I need to get back inside, Nicholas. I'll get a chill. I'll try and make you some stew tomorrow."

"Yeah, you do that."

He heard the door close quietly.

Even though he was sitting on a tree stump on a hill overlooking a colorful mesa below—even though with the nippy air everything felt open and fresh and clean—he felt claustrophobic. He was already in his coffin—the grave of a bad marriage, of a job he'd come to hate, and of the demands of a man who could put him behind bars.

And then it came to him.

True, he couldn't help Harold Bates escape, but he could get Bates to tell him where that hundred thousand was hidden. One hundred thousand dollars. He could drift down to Mexico and buy a nice place on the ocean. That kind of money could last him the rest of his life if he was careful.

He'd tried all sorts of ways to wiggle and waggle Bates's secret out of him. None had worked. But there was one method he'd always overlooked. He could beat it out of him. There were places in the prison where he could take Bates and work him over until he told Rafferty where the money was.

Packing his saddlebags with that kind of knowledge, Rafferty could ride out, find the money and start a whole new life for himself.

He took a pull on his pint. His border collie came trotting out of the woods just then, coming right over to her master. Such a sweet animal. Slender and pretty and obedient. Just like somebody else that Rafferty used to know.

He stroked the animal's back and the hootch started taking its toll on his senses. His plan to beat the information out of Bates began to shine in his mind. It would work, he thought with great excitement. Bates didn't want to die. Hell no, he didn't. Given a choice between revealing his secret and ending his life—well, it wasn't hard to imagine that Bates wouldn't hold out for very long.

He slept on the floor that night. He was sick of her noises, her smells, her clumsy apologies. Yessir, find some nice young girls in Mexico and be born again, baptized in a whorehouse ceremony with an entire harem standing by.

After returning from the prison, Fargo had spent his time waiting in his hotel room to hear from Devol and give him the news that Bates had no intention of saving his daughter by revealing where the money was hidden.

Fargo cleaned his guns, his boots, his saddlebags, throwing out about half the junk he'd accumulated for no particular reason. He had many virtues, he often joked, but tidiness was not to be found among them.

Then he sat in the rocking chair next to the window and rolled himself a cigarette. He drank a little whiskey and watched night make the small town appear much bigger

41

and more exciting than it really was. Judging by the voices drifting up from the town's three saloons, most folks hereabouts were having one hell of a good time.

When the knock came, Fargo took the Colt from his lap and aimed it directly at the door. "I'm pretty damned tired of waitin' for you."

"What the hell're you talkin' about?"

"Branson?"

"Hell no, it's not Branson. Don't wish that on me. It's Sheriff Plummer."

"Oh. C'mon in."

"That's what I was about to do."

He swung the door open and then stood in the doorway, his gun hand dropping to his holster. "I generally don't like to walk into rooms where somebody's holding a gun on me."

"I thought you were somebody else."

"Yeah, Branson."

Fargo set the Colt back on his lap. The lawman came in and leaned against the wall next to the bureau and proceeded to light himself a cigarette. "You gonna get the lamp going?"

"I like the dark."

Plummer shrugged and went on rolling his cigarette. "Funny you'd think I was Branson."

"Yeah? How come that's funny?"

"Because I'm looking for him, too."

"How come?"

"How come you went to the prison today?"

"Your deputy tell you that?"

"No, a warden named Grieves did. He also said you roughed up Rafferty. You got to be careful of Rafferty, Fargo. I know your reputation but he's got one thing on his side you don't."

"What would that be?"

Plummer grinned in the dying light. "He's crazy. You get him mad enough, he'll do anything." He flicked a lucifer with his thumb and brought the match to the cigarette dangling from the corner of his mouth. "You're a fool to get involved in this, Fargo. And I don't think you're a fool."

" 'This' being what, exactly?"

"You tell me."

"Meaning you don't know?"

"Meaning," Plummer said, "I don't know exactly. But I've got a pretty good idea. Branson and Devol served time because of Harold Bates. Bates and them were involved in the bank robbery that got them a hundred thousand dollars. Bates hid the money. They want the money. I don't know how or why they got you involved but I'm warning you they're nobody to fool with. Branson, especially. He's just as mean as Rafferty and almost as crazy." The smoke he exhaled was light blue in the deeper blue of the early darkness.

Fargo figured he had nothing to lose now. His part in the matter was over. "They kidnapped Bates's daughter. Said they'd kill her if Bates didn't tell me where the money is hid."

Fargo told him the rest, too.

Plummer laughed huskily. "I know it ain't funny, the kidnapping and all, but you must've been shocked when Bates told you they could go ahead and kill her for all he cared."

"Branson and Devol mustn't have known that Bates found out about his daughter double-crossing him that way."

"So now what? For you, I mean?"

Fargo rocked twice. The runners squeaked against the wooden floor. "Now I tell them what Bates told me and then I ride on."

"You don't think they'll hurt the girl?"

"Why would they? There's nothing to gain by it. Like I said, they probably didn't know that Bates hates his daughter."

The lawman pushed himself off the wall. "I don't want Devol and Branson drifting around. I'll need you to testify against them, about forcing you in on this kidnapping."

Fargo shook his head. "I won't do it. I want to get out of here now, tonight if possible."

Plummer walked over to the rocking chair. Honest disappointment played on his face. "I guess I had you figured wrong, Fargo. I had you figured for being on our side. Devol and Branson'll kill somebody innocent pretty soon. It's just a matter of time. I figured you'd want to help me stop them before it was too late."

"Wish I could help you, Sheriff," Fargo said. "But I hope to be gone in a couple hours or so. I got tricked into this whole thing and all I want now is shut of it."

"Before I came up here, I was gonna tell you that it was a pleasure meeting the Trailsman," Plummer said. "I guess there ain't no need for that now."

He frowned and left.

Devol showed up around nine o'clock, smelling of greasy food and beer. He tripped crossing the threshold.

"Hey, it's dark in here."

"Yeah, I noticed that, Devol."

"Just the light from the street."

"Yeah."

"How come you're holdin' a gun on me?"

"Close the door and come over here."

"You sound mad."

"Do what I say or I'll get even madder."

"Don't know why you'd be mad. We're gonna cut you in for a piece of it."

"Go close the door."

Devol shrugged. He looked scared. He went to the door, closed it, and came back.

Fargo got up out of the rocking chair where he'd been dozing. He kept his gun hand filled with his Colt. The other one he drove so deep into Devol's gut he damned near touched the man's spine.

"Oh shit," Devol said, sinking to his knees. "I'm gonna puke."

"You puke, you're gonna clean it up."

Devol spent a few minutes choking down vomit. It was close but he finally conquered it. It took a long struggle to get to his feet.

"What happened?"

"You dumb bastards didn't bother to find out that Bates knew all about Callie throwin' in with you two and double-crossing him."

"How the hell would he have found that out?"

"How the hell would I know?"

"You tell him we were gonna kill her if he didn't come through?"

"I sure did. And you know what he did?"

44

"What?"

"He laughed."

"Aw no, Fargo. He wouldn't laugh about his own daughter bein' killed."

"He may not be the sentimental old guy you two think he is. I think you could shoot her right in front of him and he wouldn't do anything about it."

"Shit," Devol said. "Branson sure won't want to hear this."

"Where's Branson now?"

"He said not to tell you."

"He did, huh? You want to get hit in the stomach again?"

"You'll just hit me. The mood Branson's in—the way you messed up his face and all—he'll shoot me."

Fargo had to make a quick decision. He could work on Devol until the man talked, but the easiest way around would be to let him go and then trail him. Callie was probably being held in a location that would be difficult to find without very clear directions.

"Get out."

"What?"

"Get out. Now. Go tell Branson what happened. And tell him I'm not carrying any more messages no matter what happens. In fact, I'll be leaving town tonight. I'm done with this whole thing."

"You're passin' up a lot of money."

"I'm not passing up anything. Bates'll never tell you where the money is. Not when the three of you were going to double-cross him. Now get going."

Devol looked almost pathetic shuffling toward the door. "This was all s'posed to be so damned easy."

"Yeah, well, it sure didn't work out that way, did it?"

"His own daughter. You just can't figure a man like that, can ya?" he said, sliding his hand over the knob. "Branson really would kill her, you know."

"She know that?"

Devol shrugged. "She's one of them little gals figures she can get any man she meets to do what she wants. She's known Branson for a long time but she still don't know him, if you understand. She thinks he's one way but he's another. She thinks she can con him into doing whatever she needs done. But she's wrong. You bring money into it, he'll kill anybody that gets in his way."

"I can see why you hang out with him."

Devol actually laughed. "I probably make him sound worse than he is. Well, I guess I don't. I seen him kill people for hardly no reason at all."

"Get out of here, Devol. I'm sick of listening to ya."

Devol, defeated, shrugged and trudged out of the room and down the hall.

6

He was like a woman, Callie Bates thought.

Branson had spent the daylight hours outdoors. He'd go for little walks but he'd always take that little mirror with him. She knew what he was doing—doting on the hot-coffee wounds Fargo had inflicted on him. They weren't even that bad. He could grow a beard and cover them up entirely.

He didn't say anything to Callie. He just sulked, or muttered to himself, sitting at the rickety table in the one-room cabin next to the creek.

But Devol had explained to her why anything that "ruined" Branson's looks was so threatening to him. Branson had grown up one of three brothers. His older brothers were rugged men with theatrically good looks. One of them, in fact, worked as an entertainer on a major steamship line. Branson's mother had always punished him by telling him how ugly he was to the point that, even though he was really just an average looking boy, he saw in the mirror somebody who was almost deformed.

It was for that reason, Devol said, you couldn't talk any sense to him. He planned to kill Fargo, no matter what, once they got her old man to tell them where the money was.

Now that it was night, she was struggling with her own demons. She had the opposite problem of Branson's. Because of her startling, sweet good looks she'd always been able to convince everybody that she was this lost innocent who badly needed help to survive the vicissitudes of life.

And God did they help. The women responded to her as they would their own child or sister. The men were not so selfless. They wanted to taste the sweet wine of her womanhood, and they'd do damned near anything to have that privilege.

She was a little worried about Branson, though, given his present mood. She'd sensed, the night before the robbery, that her father had snuck up on the three of them talking. Had he known that she, too, his own flesh and blood, was double-crossing him?

She probably should have mentioned her fears to Branson and Devol, instead of letting Fargo go to the prison and tip their hand, letting her father know officially that they were trying to get the money. Her father had enough other cash to hire killers and have all three of them wiped out. If he knew anything about her plotting against him—her father was the kind who'd kill his own daughter without hesitation.

She lighted the lamp. She lay on the cot smoking the cigarette she'd rolled for herself. All she wanted to do was get her hands on that cash, kill Branson and Devol, and head for California where she planned to have nothing but fun for many long years to come.

The door opened. Branson came in, a tall man with a wide, strong body. He kept his hat low and his head dipped so that she couldn't see his face.

He went over to the table and poured himself a drink of whiskey.

"You going to say hello or anything?" she said.

"I got things on my mind."

She rolled over on her side so she could see him. She inhaled deeply of her cigarette. You could hear night now, all the animals in the nearby woods, the creek in back and the frogs and the night birds. The cabin was cool. The birds sounded lonely.

"Branson, those marks on your face, they'll be gone in no time."

"He disfigured me."

"Oh listen to you. So solemn and everything. He didn't disfigure you. He threw some hot coffee in your face. Most people wouldn't even notice it." She wanted to reassure him so that he'd trust her enough to do what she said—right before she betrayed him. "You're just makin' too big a thing of this."

"Am I?" he snapped and turned to face her. "You're beautiful. People fall at your feet. But I'm ugly. Some people look away from me when they see me."

She laughed. "What an imagination you have, Branson! You're an average, ordinary looking man. You ain't beautiful, I'll give you that, but you sure ain't ugly, either. You sure don't seem to hurt for female companionship."

"Whores. I pay them."

"Not all of them you don't."

"Well, some of them must feel sorry for me. That's all I can figure out. I sure don't know why else they'd take up with me, even for a night."

She paused and smiled at him. "You ever think that maybe I'd like to spend a little time with you?"

"Sure you would, Callie. And that'd be because you'd want something from me, something you couldn't get no other way."

"You have a pretty low opinion of me."

"I've seen you in action, lady. I know what you're all about."

"Well, you know where you can shove that, mister. Here I try and be nice—"

But he was obviously sick of her little game. He grabbed the bottle and got up from the table so quickly, he damned near knocked it over. "Where the hell's Devol?"

"Where the hell's Fargo, you mean. He's the one who talked to my old man. He's the one I want to talk to."

Branson was at the door. He looked back at her. "Maybe you'll have to do a little sweet talkin' with him."

She gave him her best whore smile. "You don't think I'd mind that, do you? There's a man could have just about any woman he wanted."

"Yeah?" he said. "Well, wait till I get a little money in my pocket. Then we'll see who gets the women. And the pretty ones, too."

She laughed. "You'd be stupid enough to fall for their lines, too. Couple minutes ago I almost had you sweet-talked into thinkin' you weren't ugly, Branson. But let me tell you—me and most other women I've known get the willies every time you come around. You're one of the ugliest people God ever put on this earth."

She'd expected—wanted—him to be furious. Instead he

said, in a weary voice, "At least you're tellin' me the truth now."

He took the bottle and went outside.

Devol was the last of the losers. Before returning to the cabin, he spent nearly an hour in a saloon beering up for the ride back.

Fargo waited impatiently in an alley across the street, sitting his Ovaro stallion, rolling one cigarette after another, sometimes waving a hand to fan the smoke away from his face.

Devol was weaving pretty badly when he left the saloon. He spent a comical couple of minutes trying to mount up. His horse, tied to the hitching post in front of the saloon, glanced back at its rider a couple of times as if it understood how dumb the man was.

Several times in the next forty minutes, Devol damned near slipped out of the saddle. Fargo was afraid the man would fall off his mount and then he would have to go and set him back on it.

At a couple of points Devol paused, gaping around as if he'd forgotten where he was or where he was going. Or both.

None of this increased Fargo's admiration for men who'd given their lives to crime. Too often they were like Devol, amateurs. Only amateurs would think you could break the law time and time again and not get caught.

They ended up following a narrow trail along a slow-moving river. The dark water gleamed blue in the moonlight. A raccoon made his squat way across a muddy log along the shore, slipping a little every once in a while. It was a lot more fun watching the raccoon than watching Devol.

The cabin turned out to be an ancient log box in great disrepair. There was a lone window on the west side of the door but it was covered from inside with a red blanket. There was an outhouse that had been knocked over, probably in a storm, and never righted again. There was a shed but its roof had been lifted off, again probably in a storm.

"Where the hell you been?" Branson called long before Devol actually reached him. Branson occupied a tree stump, drinking rotgut from a bottle and smoking a corncob pipe.

Devol hadn't sobered up any and obviously Branson

didn't have any trouble seeing this, even from many yards away. "You sonofabitch, you're drunk. And where the hell's Fargo?"

When Devol spoke, his words were so slurred Branson leapt up from the tree stump, flung down his bottle, and went racing across the distance between them. He jumped up to yank his partner from his saddle and then hurled him to the ground with the same force he used with the whiskey bottle.

Devol cried out in pain and drunken confusion.

Fargo watched this from a stand of trees to the north of the cabin, the two figures rolling around on the ground now, in and out of the moonlight, shadows mostly. He thought of what Sheriff Plummer had said, that Branson and Devol would kill a few innocents before they made their way back to prison, or more likely the gallows. They were of a breed, these two. They couldn't even get along with each other.

Fargo eased down from his horse. He'd give it a few minutes and then he'd make his move on them. By then they'd be worn out from their brawling and they'd be easy to take.

He was scarcely finished with this thought when the world came to an abrupt end.

He had just enough time to realize that whoever had snuck up behind him knew what he was doing. He'd waited till Fargo was on the ground. Hadn't made the mistake of taking him down from the saddle. And he'd made his stride long enough that it had only taken a step or two to reach Fargo. Fargo had heard the step and started to turn but there had been no time to do anything except be aware of the pain exploding across his entire head. The bastard had used some kind of heavy batlike instrument to do his work.

Then there was just blackness, blankness, nothing.

Three hours earlier, right after suppertime, Rafferty said good-bye forever to his wife Bronwyn and the child she carried. She didn't know this, of course. He finished the jerky and biscuits he'd fixed up for himself—shit, this was the same kind of grub you got on a cattle drive; he might as well bed down on the hard ground tonight—went to the bedroom door and said, "I'm going now."

"You get enough to eat?"

"Yeah, a feast."

"I'm just so tired."

"I'm not. I work twelve hours a day six days a week and I'm never tired because I get all this good grub at home."

"You're always so angry."

And you're always such a lazy, whining bitch, he thought. "Well, like I said, I'm going."

She was halfway through asking him when he'd be back when the front door slammed.

This morning, he'd assigned one of his guards to follow Devol. The outlaw might have some ideas about springing one of the convicts and Rafferty wanted to know where he was working. The guard, young and bored, was happy to spend half the day on horseback, enjoying the freedom. He reported back to Rafferty that Devol was staying at the old cabin near what was called Indian Hill because there were two ancient burial mounds on a hill overlooking the creek.

After Rafferty left home for the final time, he went to the saloon where he spent his time. He had two whiskeys and a beer. He wanted to wait for full dark before he rode out to the cabin. He had already figured out what he wanted to do, and was anxious.

At midpoint on the ride out, he crested a hill and saw that he was following Fargo and that Fargo was following Devol. At any other time, this would have struck Rafferty as funny. One of those strange coincidences that sometimes happen to show you just how haphazard and unpredictable life really is.

What they had here was a parade, he thought sourly.

He gave the men a bit of leeway. By the time he reached the flat where the cabin stood, Devol and Branson, both of whom Rafferty remembered all too well from prison, were wrestling around on the ground. Branson was a maniac. It wasn't that he was a killer that bothered Rafferty, it was that he was reckless. He killed for no reason at all other than mood or ego, and that made him the most dangerous animal of all. A man who killed for a sound purpose—for greed, say—he was somebody you could trust enough to throw in with if necessary. Killing was part of doing business, not a fit of insanity.

He had no trouble clubbing Fargo with the billy club—just then a noisy wind rattled through the trees, covering any noise his two steps might make. The club was reinforced with a steel shank up its center. You could kill a man with a single blow, but he didn't want Fargo dead. He needed him for what he had in mind.

Branson and Devol were done fighting—Branson was dragging the other man into the cabin. Muzzy lantern light filled the doorway, and Rafferty heard a woman's voice say something from inside.

He stood behind a shaggy pine in the front yard and checked over his shotgun. He felt nothing, no fear, no excitement. He just wanted to get on with it.

He walked calmly to the half-opened door, and kicked it so hard that it fell inward. The cabin was small and messy. There was no place for either Branson or Devol to run. The girl was screaming even before he did anything.

He got Branson full on in the face. Devol he shot in the left temple.

In Rafferty's experience, people didn't just drop down and die. There were usually long moments of agony. Some cried, some moaned, some vomited, some begged, some even prayed out loud. There were twitches, lurches, spasms; there was blood and feces and urine; and then there was that moment when the entire body shuddered and settled into death. The dying part was over. Now there was just the fleshy form of what had been or what could have been but was no longer. Just another piece of meat, no different from a squirrel or a possum.

For a long, smoke-choked time, you couldn't hear the girl scream because of the shotgun blasts. But then it was all you could hear. It was like to drive him crazy.

She had jumped up on the cot and was so hysterical that she was literally trying to crawl up the cabin wall backward, just tearing her nails bloody on the coarse wood.

"You gonna kill me?" she said.

"No," he said, "I'm gonna have fun with ya. Then you're gonna help make both of us rich."

She was so eager to live that she tore her own clothes off and did all sorts of things without him even having to ask.

*　　*　　*

Thanks to Callie's tending, Fargo came to a little over an hour later. He had never had a headache to equal this one. Even opening his eyes was an ordeal.

Before he got them open, his nose hinted at what he would see. Carnage. The air was filthy with the stench of bodies that had exploded in death.

Callie said, "Don't try to move. He hit you pretty hard."

Fargo wasn't up to playing tough guy. He didn't even try to sit up. "Who got killed?"

"Yeah, the smell's pretty bad."

"So who's dead?" he snapped.

"Branson and Devol. Branson's no loss but I always felt sort of sorry for Devol."

"Who killed them?"

He heard two steps on the dirt floor. He had one eye open. A familiar face leaned in so Fargo could see it.

"I killed them, Fargo. And I'll kill you and Callie here if you don't do exactly what I say. You're going to need a day to get your strength back, then we're going after that money."

"Money?" Fargo said. Without realizing what he was doing, he tried to raise himself up from the cot. The pain was a blinding lash across his senses. For a moment, it was as if his entire body had quit him. He thought he was headed into the cold darkness again.

Callie's hand touched his cheek. It was warm, female and comforting. "You don't try that again, Fargo. You're in bad shape, believe me."

He drifted into sleep. He had no idea how long he was out and felt no better when he woke up. He opened both eyes, and, instinctively, raised a shoulder off the cot, but caught himself in time.

"Are you over there, Callie?"

"Yes."

"Is Rafferty still here?"

"I'm not going anywhere," Rafferty said.

"They really stink, Rafferty," Callie said. "I can't take this much longer. They're dead people. That don't seem to make any difference to you."

"Just a couple of hick con jobs is all they were," Rafferty said, sounding amused. "If they'd been decent people, maybe they wouldn't stink so bad."

"Decent people like you, I suppose," Callie said bitterly.

"How we going to get the money when we don't even know where it is?" Fargo said.

"Oh we'll find out where it is, all right. And you're gonna help me."

"If you're thinking of using Callie here, it won't work. Bates wouldn't go for it."

"I didn't say anything about her, Fargo. I said you were gonna help me."

"Yeah. And just how am I gonna do that?"

Rafferty said, "You're gonna break him out of prison."

7

Warden Grieves was reading and signing letters. That was the part of this job he hated the most, all the correspondence that came his way. There seemed to be at least three or four commissions he was responsible to, and then there were all the plaintive letters from spouses of the convicts. They were always trying to get their men out of prison by concocting fabulous stories, usually having to do with "new evidence" that never panned out when the letter writer was visited by a state lawyer.

Jimmy knocked, peeked in, and said, "Mrs. Rafferty's here to see you, Warden."

"Mrs. Rafferty? Hmm. What the hell does she want? Well, show her in." He rarely felt as harassed and as sorry for himself than when he was writing letters. While he was thankful for a break in the routine, he resented her because she would obviously distract him from finishing writing his letters.

Having been a warden for so many years, Grieves had a sense of when an unexpected visitor would bring good or bad news, and with this visit sensed bad news. Perhaps very bad news.

She'd been a pretty little thing back when Grieves and his wife had come to the prison. Now she was no longer pretty nor little. This wasn't a result of the pregnancy. The popular conception was that some people just "let themselves go." While Grieves thought that was likely true in some cases, he felt that in many others the beauty of youth simply vanished from certain people, and there wasn't a damned thing they could do about it. Poor Mrs. Rafferty was one of them.

After she was seated and they exchanged the proper cordialities, she said, "I think my husband may have deserted me, Warden."

"Deserted you? Well, what makes you think that?"

"He didn't come home last night and he hasn't come to work here yet."

Warden Grieves didn't want to appear as if he didn't know that his chief guard was absent. "Yes, I know he's late. I assumed he had a good reason."

"The good reason," she said, and began to weep with great unnerving fervor, "is that he deserted me because I'm fat and ugly now and I didn't make him his meals no more."

Grieves was thankful that she'd mentioned meals because that gave him something to talk about. Fat and ugly, there was nothing he could say. Now making meals—there you had something. "Well, that's something you can fix up, isn't it, Mrs. Rafferty? A man needs a good meal in the evening. Especially a man who works as hard as your husband does."

Grieves's patience was nearing its end. The only problem women had that interested him was when they said that they'd missed their monthly time. Thank God there were plenty of abortion mills all over the West.

"But being around food when I'm pregnant like this—it makes me sick."

He almost laughed. A balloon of a woman this size—sick around food? Unlikely.

Another knock. Jimmy again. "Rafferty's here now. He wants to see you."

"Well, send him in," Warden Grieves said in his most commanding manner. "I want to see him, too. As does his wife."

As soon as Rafferty came into the room, he saw her sitting there and his face went white. Rafferty rarely lost control for even a moment, but he lost this moment entirely. He started to stammer.

Grieves said, "Sit down, Rafferty. This little lady seems to be in need of listening—you listening to her. And then both of you listening to me."

Fargo was right where Rafferty had left him, bound ankle and wrist on the cot, without the energy to slip from his bonds. He had long periods of lucidity now. He realized that he was suffering from a concussion. He had suffered such before. They took time to right themselves and there was no cure but time.

He raised his head twice, at painful expense, to glimpse Callie stuffed in the corner of the cabin. Bound ankle, wrist, and gagged.

Fargo slipped in and out of consciousness.

He lived mostly in fever dreams, mentally crisscrossing various timelines in his life. He spoke to people he'd cared about but hadn't seen in years; cursed people who'd betrayed him in one way or another; apologized to people he'd inadvertently hurt or let down in some way; and had a picture of himself as an older man retired on a farm in Missouri. There were dreams of lust as his loins led him down corridors filled with various women he'd bedded.

His longest, most lustful dream was of a woman named Jacqueline from the boisterous Cajun section of New Orleans.

Fargo had been hired by a local politician as a bodyguard. The man was one of the few honest politicos in the entire county; therefore, he was targeted for death so that one of the crooks could take his seat. And there would be no worry about the crooked type winning at the ballot box. The election was all taken care of. Hundreds of dead folks would be voting—and guess who they'd be voting for?

Fargo saved the man's life twice and saw to it that he got reelected. The man had a beautiful twenty-year-old daughter named Jacqueline.

Now that his job was done, Fargo was eager to start roaming again. He put into a hotel for the night, planning to board his Ovaro stallion on a steamship and have himself some fun drinking, gambling, and womanizing.

The womanizing started earlier than he'd anticipated.

Sometime near midnight there came a soft knock on the door of his hotel room. Before he could get out of bed to reply, he heard a key slip in place, and then the door was opened.

Backlit by the hall sconces, Jacqueline presented a fetching and dramatic silhouette. She wore a floor-length cape that fell away from her before she'd quite closed the door.

For a moment he saw her tall regal body as a voluptuous shadow.

She made herself a gift to him that night, a perfumed, silken-skinned, eager gift that began the festivities by pressing him gently back on the bed and kissing his mouth, then patiently kissing him all the way down to his groin. She took his ample manhood in her knowing mouth, stroking him with a cat-lazy tongue in an effort to tease him to full hardness, and then covered him with her mouth.

She brought him right to the verge of exploding before pulling away so that she could lie back and guide him inside her. She groaned with enormous appetite and satisfaction when she felt his massive ramrod fill her and pry deeper and deeper as they found a mutual rhythm so violent this first time around, the bed threatened to collapse.

Afterward, she joked that he had violated every orifice of her body—and that she loved it. And that was virtually true. Three, four, five times during that endless carnal night he took her front, back, and with her sitting on his lap so that she could use him like a sexual appliance. He didn't mind being used that way at all, especially since he got to fill his hands with her wondrously fleshed buttocks and his mouth with her wondrously fleshed breasts.

Their last tryst was just before dawn, with both of them on the floor, with her hind end stuck way up in the air and him mounting her from behind; and then her rolling over on her hip so that he could take her from the side, sliding into her hot juicy sex at the only angle they hadn't tried that night.

He groaned in his sleep now, recalling that long-ago New Orleans night. He awoke to a cold joyless cabin, lashed with rope, head still hurting but at least not to the degree that it had twelve hours earlier. There was still no real strength in his arms or hands. Not enough, anyway, to make it possible for him to slip his bonds and escape.

He wanted warmth, food, and coffee. But most of all he wanted vengeance on a man named Rafferty—a man he would kill, and soon. There was no doubt about that now. No other alternative would satisfy him, certainly not money. Fargo was about honor, not greed, and Rafferty had dishonored him many times over.

*　　*　　*

The session with Warden Grieves lasted nearly an hour. Grieves delivered a sermon on the sanctity of marriage. Bronwyn wept, which seemed to please Grieves a great deal—it was one way of assessing his effectiveness—while Rafferty tried hard not to look bored. Grieves had become a decent public speaker over the years, often lecturing on law and order, and listening carefully to good orators and preachers to pick up their rhythms and cadences. He'd learned one amazing secret—that sometimes it mattered more how you said it than what you said.

At the end, Grieves said, "Now do you two have anything to say to each other?" He wanted, expected, and silently demanded a big clinch and pledges of undying love. Bronwyn was no trouble. Rafferty had to do some of the best playacting he'd ever done. He just wanted to get the hell out of here. He'd only stopped in here to pick up his pay, which came twice a month. He'd need it when he went looking for the gold. Bronwyn would have to worry about herself. She had kin all around these parts. They'd take care of her.

Rafferty knew he had to make it look good. "I'll be back, Warden. I'll just walk her to the gate."

"See," Grieves said merrily, "it's working already."

"Oh, Warden, Warden," Bronwyn gushed. "Thank you so much."

This was one of the longest walks in Rafferty's life. Bronwyn clung to him, cooing all those irritating little lovey-dovey things she used to coo back when he was still trying to get into her knickers—knickers worth getting into in those days. He did his best to respond, patting her arm, kissing the top of her head.

At the gate, she said, "I'm going to make you a very special supper tonight, just like Warden Grieves said I should."

"I'd really appreciate that."

"And I'll leave it up to you about last night."

"Last night?"

"Yes. You know, if you want to tell me where you spent the night."

"Oh. Yes."

"Maybe you think it's not any of my business."

"Well."

"Or maybe you think it'd be better to wait until you got home tonight and we could talk it over at the dinner table. If you have anything to confess—anything—I'm almost positive I can forgive you, honey."

"That's very nice of you."

"Unless you don't think it's any of my business, honey. But then maybe you should think on what the warden said about trust and all."

"I'll be doin' a lot of thinkin', honey," he said, the word "honey" like ant poison on his tongue. She walked through the gate, and he headed back to the warden's to get his check.

Jimmy, the warden's man at the desk in the reception area, said, "He's busy."

"He wasn't busy five minutes ago."

"Well, he's busy now."

Jimmy loved it when he could push guards around. If he was planning to stay around longer, Rafferty would have made a point of pushing Jimmy around right now. Real hard.

Rafferty wasn't just surprised who came out of the warden's office, he was downright shocked. Harold Bates looked as surprised to see Rafferty as Rafferty was to see him.

Rafferty wondered what the hell Bates had been talking to the warden about, and he damned well meant to find out. Not here, not now, but very soon.

Rafferty stalked into the warden's office. "I need to get my pay, sir."

The warden opened one of his desk drawers, and took out a sheet of lined paper that each employee had to sign to get his pay. He pushed it over to Rafferty. Rafferty signed and pushed it back.

The warden handed him his check. "You buy that little wife of yours somethin' nice."

"I sure will."

"I just hope my little talk did some good."

Rafferty was already at the door. "It did a lot of good, Warden. And thanks."

He caught up with Bates right before the convict reached the blacksmith shop.

"What the hell were you talking to the warden about, Bates?"

Bates squinted into the hot sun. "None of your business."

"The hell."

"You going to beat me up right out here, are you, Rafferty?"

"What the hell were you talking about, I said?" Rafferty grasped Bates's flabby arm with enough force to lift the smaller man off his heels.

"I told him I wanted the other cell block."

There were two cell blocks and each block had its own chief guard.

"What the hell's this all about?" Rafferty said.

"Well, if you won't help me break out, maybe Gibbons will." Bates smiled. "You better go easy on me, Rafferty. Here come some of them church women."

Two of the ladies who always brought special pastries were walking toward them, escorted by a guard with a shotgun. They were certain to be interested in why such a big man as Rafferty was manhandling somebody as small as Bates.

Rafferty startled Bates by smiling. "Well guess what, little man?"

"What's so funny?"

"You are. You got so het up about bustin' out you forgot somethin'."

"Yeah? Like what?"

"Like how I always take care of you one way or the other."

"What's that supposed to mean?"

"It means that Skye Fargo's going to be here tomorrow and he's gonna help you bust."

Now it was Bates who smiled. "Well, I'll be damned, Rafferty." He sounded almost admiring of the man he considered a killer and little else. "I'll be damned."

8

By the following morning, Skye Fargo had regained enough strength to go out to the creek and give himself a cold bath and a shave.

The water baptized him. He was born again to strength and purpose. Soon enough he was going to overpower Rafferty and kill him. For now, for the sake of the girl, he had no choice but to play along.

He thought several times of sneaking back up to the cabin and stealing the girl from Rafferty. But he was reluctant for a simple reason. Rafferty sat directly across from Callie, his gun on her. He'd given Fargo ten minutes to take his bath and get back to the cabin. If Fargo tried in any way to rescue the girl, he would undoubtedly get her killed. Rafferty was simply that kind of man.

Rafferty, who'd kept both Fargo and Callie tied up all night—putting Skye on the floor so that Rafferty himself could enjoy the dubious comforts of the cot—had hot coffee going by the time Fargo returned.

The coffee smell almost made things normal. Fargo felt as if he'd spent the last forty-eight hours in some kind of coffin, drifting in and out of reality while his concussion began its slow healing process. He went into the cabin and sat down across from Rafferty.

"You remember everything I told you?"

Fargo smiled bitterly. "If I'm as dumb as you seem to think I am, Rafferty, why do you want to use me in the first place?"

"No way you're dumb, Fargo. But I just want to make sure you got everything down."

"Oh, I got it down all right, Rafferty. The only thing you

haven't explained is what if the warden decides to just kill both me and Bates."

Rafferty grinned. "Then I guess your luck runs out."

Fargo went over and stood above Callie. Her eyes begged him to be set free of her bonds and the gag that was cutting into her mouth. He looked back at Rafferty. "I don't do anything unless you untie her and let her go down to the creek and wash up and then have some of that coffee."

"And what if I don't?"

"Then I can guarantee that things won't go so good at the prison. And you won't get your money."

Rafferty shrugged. "Untie her, then."

Callie's eyes reflected the joy she felt. Being tied up was something that happened to the hero in every dime novel ever printed, but few writers reflected the reality of prolonged imprisonment of this kind. After a day or so, the body started to shut down various processes. The prisoner had to urinate, circulation was cut off, and even when set free, walking wasn't easy at first. One was wobbly and weak, just as Callie was when Fargo had stripped her of her bonds. She'd been on her feet only a few seconds when she pitched forward into Fargo's arms. Fargo steadied her. "Give her some coffee," he snapped.

"Yessir, boss man," Rafferty said. "I sure wouldn't want to disappoint you, now would I?"

Fargo figured Rafferty for a man who would sacrifice his pride in order to get what he wanted. Toting coffee wasn't something he'd do ordinarily but if it moved him closer to that one hundred thousand dollars, he'd sure as hell do it. No sense wasting time on some trivial argument. Just get the coffee and shut up about it.

Fargo got Callie seated at the table. She'd need a few minutes before she was ready to walk down to the creek. She drank the coffee lustily. It was the first nourishment—if you could call it that—that she'd had in many hours. Fargo poured a cup for himself.

Rafferty said, "Don't kill anybody unless absolutely necessary."

"Thanks for the advice."

"You kill somebody, that'll double the number of posses

that come after us. Busting Bates out'll bring posses enough. Probably two or three."

Fargo looked at Rafferty. "You might not believe this, Rafferty, but I don't go around killing people."

"You've done your share."

"When I was forced to. And I sure as hell don't plan on killing anybody at the prison. I'll get him out for you and then he's all yours." He glanced at Callie, who was still working her way through the steaming cup of coffee. "She's all yours, too. Unless she gets smart and walks away from the whole thing. You and Bates deserve each other. There's still some hope for Callie."

"I want the money, Fargo," Callie said, pausing long enough with her coffee to talk. "My old man never did anything for me. He barely acknowledged I was even around. He owes me lots of things. But the only way I can get satisfaction is to get money from him. Because money is all he cares about."

Rafferty smiled. "Smart man."

"Yeah, you'd think so, wouldn't you, Rafferty?" she said. "That's because you're just like him. You're walking out on your wife and kid and you don't give a damn at all. Same as my old man did. That's why he's got to pay. For what he did to my mom and me. And I'm gonna see that he does pay, too."

That was when Fargo moved. Rafferty had let himself get involved in what Callie was saying. A mistake. A bad one. When Rafferty turned from Callie to see what Fargo was up to, Fargo splashed scalding coffee in Rafferty's face.

But what had worked so well with Branson the other night at the campfire didn't work so well here. Rafferty had time—all he needed was a second—to raise his arm enough to block the brown steaming wave of coffee headed for his face. The back of his forearm caught the worst of it. His sleeve was soaked but that was about the only damage.

He moved swiftly. He obviously didn't want to reinjure Fargo's head. Fargo needed all his senses to pull off the prison break.

Rafferty compromised. Instead of damaging Fargo's head, he injured his groin, bringing up the toe of his Texas boot deep into Fargo's crotch.

Fargo was reduced to a pile of gasps and groans on the floor next to where Callie had been tied up.

Once a week Warden Grieves visited Harold Bates to the great amusement of the other convicts. Even the warden had to come sniffing around all that money. He claimed to visit Bates because Bates needed a certain kind of sinus medication that was available in town. The warden picked it up for him at the apothecary every week. Kind of funny, of course, that the warden wouldn't ever do any other inmate a favor like this. Not under any circumstances.

Grieves walked into the blacksmith area of the large barn. Bates was shoeing a horse. Crazy Dutch Prentiss wasn't around. Just as well. Dutch Prentiss scared the hell out of everyone in this prison, including Grieves.

"Brought your medicine," Grieves said to Bates. He set the small bottle on a wooden crate. "How're your sinuses this week?"

" 'Bout as bad as usual," Bates said. He sneezed as if to demonstrate his point.

Grieves let Bates finish up the shoeing before he said anything else. He spent the time thinking of a subtle way to bring up Skye Fargo's visit. A man like Fargo didn't just appear without a good reason, and he sure as hell wasn't related to Bates.

That left only one possibility as far as Grieves was concerned—the money, all that ill-gotten gain from the bank robbery. Grieves, a widower, wanted to spend his final years in the South Seas. He spent his nights reading fiction and travel essays, which dealt with life in that part of the world. Innocent young women, bountiful of body and easy of virtue, and trade winds that could make a middle-aged man feel young again. The only hitch was supporting himself in such a lifestyle. A warden just didn't make that much money. But a bank robber did. Hence, his years spent ferrying Bates's sinus medicine from drug counter to prison.

Bates knew what the warden was up to, of course. He was an intelligent man. Easy to see that Grieves wanted some sort of advantage where the money was concerned, as did damned near everybody else in this prison.

The trouble was that, as yet, Grieves hadn't figured out a plan for getting Bates to share his secret hiding place. The easiest thing would be to help Bates escape in exchange for a good share of the money. When the actual exchange took place, he could kill Bates and take it all for himself. But Bates still had not taken a liking to the man. He was always, as now, cold, giving the impression that he wanted to be as far away from the warden as possible. If Grieves ever felt that Bates had accepted him, he'd hop to making the escape offer. But the time wasn't ready yet.

"Next week's your birthday," Grieves said as he watched Bates lead the shod horse out to the rope corral and the sunshine. Grieves followed him. "Next Tuesday night, matter of fact."

"I didn't know you kept up on our birthdays," Bates said. "Every man here gets a big birthday party, does he?" Bates loved chiding him, making him feel foolish, using his own greed to humiliate him.

"I think you know better than that, Harold."

"I thought I asked you not to call me 'Harold.' "

"Say, that's right, I forgot. I'm sorry."

Damn, he hated groveling in front of a convict this way. It would be so easy to grab this little bastard by the throat and squeeze him for the secret, but he had the sense that Bates was one of those little men—little in height, not weight—who would rather die than give in.

"My friends call me 'Harold.' Everybody else calls me 'Bates.' "

"I already told you I'm sorry."

Imagine a warden playing a sniveling toady like this— humiliating. By this time, he'd humiliated himself so often in front of Bates that only every penny of the hundred thousand could possibly balm the wounds cut deep into his pride.

"Fargo told me he was your cousin."

"He did, did he?"

Grieves followed Bates inside the rope corral where six other workhorses awaited shoeing. Bates reached up and started to lead a huge plow horse from the corral. "C'mon, Old Tom," he said to the animal.

Grieves stood behind the horse. "Funny you never mentioned you being related to Fargo and all. He's got quite the reputation. He—"

Suddenly the corral was whiplashed by a stream of the vilest curses.

Bates looked to see what had happened.

Grieves's preciously shined and polished and very expensive boots had been befouled by a long brown stream of watery horse manure.

Bates laughed. "Old Tom's got quite a reputation, too. For diarrhea."

He kept on laughing and leading the horse into the smithy area. Grieves kept right on cursing.

9

Tempting to just keep riding, Fargo thought. Forget Callie, forget Rafferty. She'd lied to him and because of that he owed her nothing. As much as he hated Rafferty, vengeance would get him what? A good feeling for maybe twenty-four hours? And then what? He'd find himself in some other situation, with some other version of Rafferty. There were a lot of Raffertys in the world and they all needed killing. Fargo was only one man and no saint himself.

These were his thoughts as he came in view of the town. He'd pick up clothes and a spare gun from his hotel room and ride out to the prison. As much as he wanted to ride away from it all, he knew he couldn't leave Callie with Rafferty.

He gathered up his belongings in his room and went downstairs to pay his bill. He smiled at the two nice-looking ladies on the steps of the hotel, waving to passersby. The hotel wars must be heating up. Two beauties instead of one. Too bad he didn't have time to take advantage of them.

He was walking over to the hitching post when a familiar voice said, "Figured you'd come back for your things, Fargo."

Fargo didn't have to turn around to know that it was Sheriff Plummer. The man had a tobacco-raspy voice and a slow, intentional way of talking.

Fargo finished up stuffing his saddlebag and then turned to the lawman. "Nice day. Probably won't get to be over two hundred by noon."

Plummer smiled. "I don't believe I've heard you say a single positive thing about our little town here."

"I'm sure if I stayed here long enough, I'd find something I liked about it. Right now nothing comes to mind."

"You sure can be a hard-ass when you want to be."

Fargo's eyes narrowed. "I expect the same is true of you."

Plummer's face tightened, his smile disappearing. "Funny you should say that."

"Yeah? Why's that?"

Plummer glanced down the street. His gaze never strayed from the events of the business district. He wanted things to go along in an orderly fashion, and he'd see to it that they did. "It's funny you should mention me being a hard-ass because that's just what I'm going to be with you right now."

"Any special reason?"

"Because the warden thinks something is going on with you and Harold Bates."

"He does, huh? Why would he think that?"

Plummer shrugged. "Guess he didn't buy your story that you're Bates's first cousin."

"Second cousin."

Plummer couldn't help himself. He had to smile a little. "The mark of a good bullshitter. Always keeps his story straight. All right, Fargo, the warden doesn't buy your story that you're Bates's second cousin."

"Aunt Elly Mae'd sure be sad to hear about that."

Plummer said, "The warden's nobody to play around with."

"He tougher than you are?"

"Maybe not tougher. But meaner. A lot meaner." Again, he surveyed the street. In the gathering heat everything seemed to move slowly, as through crystal molasses, fighting heat and dust and a natural tendency to seek shade and just simply rest until night came with at least a modicum of relief. "He'll just kill you. Backshoot you if necessary. And there won't be anything I can do about it."

Fargo said, "I'm half-tempted to just ride away from it all."

"That'd be the smart thing to do. But you won't."

"Can't," Fargo said and then swung up on his Ovaro. "You going to tell me what's going on?"

This time it was Fargo who smiled. "You really wouldn't expect me to, now would you, Sheriff?"

They both had a good laugh about that one.

Fargo got his stallion turned around and rode out of town.

It was hard to tell if the prison looked more forbidding at night than day. Its massive sloping walls of stone were probably more intimidating during the lighted hours, Fargo decided, because you could see how impossible escape was.

He spent two hours in the smothering heat of the early afternoon searching all four sides of the prison with field glasses. There were enough trees to keep his presence secret, though a few times he froze when the tower guards suddenly turned in his direction. They were huge and formidable men even at this distance. Close-up in the windows of the field glasses their faces had a brute ugliness matched only by the customized shotguns they carried. One man had a double-barreled sawed-off shotgun sitting on a nearby ledge as well. They were obviously ready—and most likely eager—for any kind of grief you decided to push their way.

From what he was able to see, there was not a single way out of the prison except the front gate and the smaller door built into it, the door where he'd had his first battle with Rafferty. The plan Rafferty had devised was thus dependent on Bates's ability to stay alive long enough to cross the prison yard and reach the gate before the warden gave the order to open fire—no more negotiating, no more waiting.

That was the first flaw in Rafferty's plan. The second flaw was that Rafferty didn't think he'd be implicated in the escape because he wasn't physically present. Fargo had argued with him about this for two hours, stressing that Warden Grieves would obviously be suspicious of the guard. The day after Rafferty not only quits but deserts his wife, Harold Bates busts out? The warden wouldn't be suspicious about Rafferty engineering all this so that Bates could escape and lead him to the money? The warden would start looking for Rafferty immediately.

That was the third flaw in Rafferty's argument. The

money. Everybody wanted that damned money except Fargo. All he wanted to do was free a none-too-innocent woman of whom he felt oddly protective. She might not be innocent but she sure didn't deserve a fate that involved Rafferty. And then he just wanted to ride away. He could easily picture them all descending on the bags of money like maggots on a fresh carcass. It was an unseemly, unholy picture.

He climbed a tree in the late afternoon and from there he was able to watch the traffic that moved in and out of the gate. There was never a moment when a guard wasn't present. Distracting the night watchman wouldn't be easy. Rafferty said that the man would be under strict orders never to leave his post no matter what. The night guard had a whistle and was told to use it in case of emergency. Fargo would have to figure out some way to get close enough to the guard to overpower him and do this without getting killed. A man on night duty at a prison was going to be damned suspicious of any civilian who approached him. There was just no good reason for a private citizen to be around a prison at night.

This was where the fourth and final flaw came in. The inmates bedded down at eight thirty every night, even when the sunset was still a bloody red streaking the Texas sky. Warden Grieves had seen to it that Harold Bates had gotten the only single cell in the entire prison. This cell was isolated from the others, on the ground floor of the first building in an area where the guards took breaks. The cell was secure but it was a privilege to have because you didn't have to hear all the ugly sounds of a prison at night—the prisoners attacking each other, sobbing out of loneliness and fear, emptying their bowels and their bladders, or having the kind of sexual encounters Harold Bates, a proper gentleman in his own mind, did not like to think about.

And now the fourth flaw. One other privilege the warden had bestowed upon Harold was that even though he'd instructed the guards to let Bates walk around the empty prison yard until nine thirty, there was no guarantee that the note Rafferty had sent to Bates last night via one of the other guards had actually reached him. The note instructed Bates to be as near the front gate at nine o'clock tonight as possible.

The flaw was obvious to Fargo but not to Rafferty. What if the guard carrying the note decided to read it and then share it with the warden? Or what if he decided to read it and then be at the gate himself tonight, thus cutting himself in for a share of the money? Or what if, for some reason, Harold Bates decided that as much as he wanted to bust out, this was starting to look too much like a trap? Maybe he'd figured out, as he should have, that Rafferty was going to kill him once he learned where the money was.

Rafferty dismissed all the flaws, saying Fargo was worrying about nothing.

But when Fargo headed back to town in the late afternoon for some supper and a few beers, his mind was troubled. There was so much that could go wrong in a plan like this. And a man—let's say a man named Skye Fargo—could get killed being a part of it.

10

Warden Grieves usually stopped off for a beer at the most respectable of the saloons when he came into town at the end of the day. The official residence at the prison was being refurbished following a fire of suspicious nature. Grieves had a good idea who did it but he wanted confirmation from a snitch before he moved on the inmate responsible. He'd nearly killed a man with his own fists last year and the state authorities took notice of the incident. Thus, Grieves was visited frequently by various representatives of do-gooder groups. This arson case he'd have to handle officially to show everybody that he was being a good lad. Governmental groups liked people who at least pretended to be good lads.

Grieves stayed at a boarding house where the food was good, the widow who ran it had exotic tastes in sex, and where he had half the entire floor upstairs.

But the before-supper beers had become something of a ritual over the past five weeks so here he was now at the bar, listening to some of the local businessmen complain about anything they could. One homburg'd fellow even gave a testy little speech about how he couldn't buy a pair of shoes that did jack shit for his fallen arches, though the man who sold shoes complained right back that size 15 DDDDD was not a foot meant to be confined in leather. Grieves got a good laugh out saying that the complainer should think of going barefoot, like a caveman.

Grieves was just ordering his third beer when somebody came up beside him and said to the bartender, "You let me pay for that one and for one of my own, Charlie."

"Appreciate the free beer."

"Be a lot more peaceable country if everybody bought everybody else free beers once in a while," Plummer said in the folksy way he sometimes talked.

"Guess I couldn't argue with that."

Grieves sensed that the lawman had something on his mind, but Plummer was a man who usually took his time to getting around to the real subject at hand. Finally, he said, "I hear you talked to a man named Fargo."

"Fargo, oh yes," Grieves said. "Kind of man I'd like to see swinging from a tree."

"Well, I wouldn't go that far. But I sure wonder what he's up to."

"So do I." Grieves then told Plummer about Fargo's trip to the prison.

"He was there again today."

"He was? I saw the visitor's list. Didn't see his name anywhere."

"I had the Pawnee trail him."

The Pawnee was a retired cavalry scout who picked up side money doing jobs for the sheriff's office. He'd been a tracker all his life.

"The way he tells it, Fargo didn't go into the prison. He stayed outside, far enough away so you couldn't see him."

"Doing what?"

Their beers came, sudsy and sumptuous.

"That's the funny thing. He spent the time checking out every wall of the prison through field glasses. Finally ended up watching the front gate for nearly an hour and a half."

Grieves sensed that things were coming clear where Fargo was concerned. He visited his "second cousin" Harold Bates in prison and then he returned to scout out the place. There could be only one reason that a man scouted out a prison exterior—to plot out the escape of somebody inside.

"You just might have some trouble on your hands," Plummer said. "I figured you'd be in here for a couple of beers so I didn't ride out to the prison. You've still got time to arrange things in case Fargo decides to make his move tonight."

Grieves smiled. "That money's like to make all of us

crazy, isn't it? One hundred thousand dollars cash and it's all we can think about. That's why Fargo's involved, of course."

"Yeah, that's sort of the way I see it, too."

"You want any help, let me know about it." Plummer finished his beer, setting his glass down on the sticky bar.

"I appreciate the offer, sheriff. I certainly do." Grieves drained his own beer. "Looks like I'd better be getting back to the prison. Guess I'll be working a little late tonight."

"You take this home to your mother," Father Thomas Michaels said, "and tell her it is God's reward for coming to mass every day of the week."

Rosarita Aranga, the fifteen-year-old considered by all to be the prettiest girl in the Texas town of Munoz, bowed to the elderly priest. She looked even more beautiful in the dancing lights of the votive candles beneath the statue of the Virgin. The red kerchief she wore over her dark hair framed the perfect features of her face. Even in a faded yellow dress and barefoot, the girl had a natural elegance that men of all ages responded to, even old men who'd taken the vow of poverty. The priest hoped the girl would travel further up the Rio Grande when she turned sixteen. She deserved a better fate than the one this small town held for her.

"You are the most generous man in all of Texas," Rosarita said, touching the sleeve of the old man's cassock. And so it was said by everybody in the town, that without Father Michaels, the people and the buildings would have fallen into dust like so many other towns had done in recent years.

She touched his one valuable possession, a ruby ring that had been given to him by a grateful and wealthy woman whom he'd counseled when her son fell into trouble. She had rewarded him with this special gift.

Roasarita held his hand up and kissed the ring. "You are the best priest we've ever had here, Father. I know this is not a blessed ring, but the people, they talk about it as if it has divine powers. Whenever we have problems, we come to you and you take care of them for us. You are not like the priest before. I should not speak ill against a man of the cloth but he did not care about us, Father. He did not care that we suffered and that some of us went hungry half the time. But you—" She smiled. "Maybe this ring is blessed, after all."

The priest who had been in Munoz before Father Michaels had been a lazy and foolish man and one who did not much like Mexican people. It was wrong to think of a prelate, everybody knew, but with this vain and intolerant man, it was all one could think. There had even been a rumor that he was seeing one of the white people of the town on the sly. Perhaps it was for this reason that the Archbishop had replaced him with Father Michaels.

Not that the people took to the new priest immediately. He was an old man with arthritis. The other one had been lazy. This one looked infirm. But he surprised everybody by reroofing the adobe church by himself in the scorching sun, and by completely changing the shape of the altar. He did not ask for help from the men because he knew they needed to work during the daylight hours. Even more than that, he helped them build adobe homes, enrich their gardens so they could eat better, and even showed the goatherds how to treat their animals when they were ailing.

Shortly after he refurbished the altar, he began dispensing money. The assumption was that the old priest came from a wealthy family. Of course nobody could be sure, and though he was generous, he was also frugal. He didn't just hand it out—one had to come to him with serious purpose in his eyes and on his lips. Father Michael's money was for true emergencies. Never for trifles nor whims. But if one's story was true and intent honest, the money needed would be given in front of the statue of the Virgin.

"You are a true friend to my people," Rosarita said, so bold as to kiss the old man on the cheek. "The other ones, or so my mother says, always favored the whites."

This was a problem all along the Rio Grande, the old priest knew. There were not enough ordained Mexicans to go around—though that was changing now—so white priests were pressed upon brown people and not always to good effect. The white priests tended to socialize and feel closest to the white members of their flock.

"The gift is from God, Rosarita. Please don't fuss over me. I'm privileged to be able to share."

She nodded modestly and then said, "I will take this to

my parents. We will take my sister to the doctor in the city now. Maybe she will not die after all."

She withdrew, leaving the prelate to stand in the heavy shadows of the church that still smelled of this morning's incense. He had always loved to sit in the ancient dark church, with only the light of the red and yellow and blue votive candles playing off the humble white statue of the Virgin.

He sat in a pew.

The money was running low. He had found the bag of it—Rock Springs Bank & Trust it had printed across its side—when he had changed the altar around. The priest before him had rebuilt the tabernacle on the altar, the box where the sacred hosts for communion were kept. When Father Michaels had lifted it up to move it along with the altar itself, he had found a dark, open space beneath the tabernacle. Far below in the dark dirt hole lay the bank bag. He pulled it up with a rake—he couldn't fish it out any other way.

His first inclination had been to walk down the dusty street to the sheriff's office and hand the bag over. But just then a little girl came down the center aisle of the church with her mother. They knelt at the communion rail and both prayed aloud for the same thing. They needed a new horse for plowing. The father had died of influenza the spring before. A horse was not expensive to most people, but to this woman it was a fortune.

That first time, giving the money to the woman, the priest had convinced himself that this would be the only time he used money from the bank bag. It was clearly money from a robbery and belonged back with its owner. As soon as the woman and the little girl left the church, he would take the remaining money to Sheriff Culhane.

Yet somehow he never made that trip. He saw the sheriff many times over the past four years but he never once brought up the subject of the bank bag, never once made mention of the money he was handing out to people.

Now there was very little left. A few dollars at most. The old priest had been scrupulous. Never a cent for himself or even for the church. The money had gone strictly to the poorest people of his flock and then for only the most compelling of needs. His flock had many needs.

From time to time the old priest wondered if the robbers would ever return to get their money. Probably not. Robbers tended to go on robbing and eventually get themselves killed. The old man saw this as a gift from God. God had put the thought of refurbishing the church in his mind so that he would come across the money and thus help his flock.

The priest just wished, as he sat there relaxing in the dark, that he had even more to give.

The prison was just settling in for the night when Fargo took up his position behind a stand of scrub pines thirty yards from the front gate. Though it was not yet full night, the sky was the color of dark blue velvet and the stars shone down with a glittering beauty.

He hated waiting—it sapped him, distracted him. It was difficult to keep his concentration when waiting started to aggravate him.

At eight, there was a changing of the guards. There was no military formality. One Mexican in khaki replaced another. A few words were exchanged, probably a joke given the way both men laughed. The relief man took up position.

From inside came a stout male voice reading a Bible passage. He read it loud enough to be heard throughout the prison. Prisons were a good place to learn the Bible, along with refining your skills at burglary, robbery, and murder.

Fargo just wanted to be done with the damned waiting.

Warden Grieves took up his position after the prayer had been read. The second building had a wooden porch that ran the length of the jail. He had placed three barrels at the east end of the porch so he could hide behind them. Otherwise Bates would be able to see him when he came out for his evening stroll.

Grieves had decided that the best thing to do was to wound Bates severely but not kill him. He would get him in the infirmary and beat him until Bates told him the whereabouts of the money.

He would let Fargo go ahead and take out the guard at the gate so that the attempted prison break would be obvious to any investigator; therefore he would be within his rights to shoot Bates.

He squatted behind the barrels. Damn, he hated waiting.

Fargo decided to climb the same tree he'd used as a lookout this afternoon. Might as well scan the interior of the prison. He'd be able to see Bates appear in the open space. He would still have plenty of time to reach the guard at the gate and knock him out.

It was just then that Fargo's gaze was directed to a wooden porch on the side of the second building. Moonlight had glinted off metal.

Fargo, even more tired of waiting, was glad that he had something to get nervous about. He'd wanted a distraction and now he had one.

Moonlight glinting off metal—a line of three barrels. The round shape that might very well be the top of a man's head.

He did not need to be a wise and learned man to see that these were the familiar elements of a classic trap.

Harold Bates lay on the cot in his cell. Sometimes at night he lit a candle to read by, but not tonight. He was sweating, sick to his stomach with fear.

Harold Bates was a man possessed of many masculine virtues. Unfortunately courage was not one of them.

Not until half an hour ago did he realize that a man— namely one Harold Edwin Bates—could get killed trying to break out of prison.

Damned right he could.

What if Fargo wasn't able to subdue the guard? The guard just might shoot both Fargo and Bates. Or what if Fargo and he managed to escape, only to be gunned down by a dog-led posse? That happened all the time. Or what happened if—

If, if, if. He hadn't thought of any of the ifs before. He'd been so fixated on his freedom that nothing else cluttered his mind, and now the ifs had started to clutter his mind.

It was that damned money—it had become his curse. It was all he thought of—and all everybody else thought of.

He swatted a fly away from the greasy sweat on his face.

Then he sat up, thinking he might get himself a drink of water.

But when he stood up he was trembling so badly that his legs would not support him. He lowered himself back to the cot.

It was seven minutes before he was to walk out of this cell and never return.

Seven more minutes of if if if.

Was he really going to break out of here tonight?

Fargo had no idea who the man on the porch was, why he had a rifle, or what he planned to do with it. It was too dark to see the man's face. Though it was obvious that the man was waiting for Harold Bates to appear, Fargo had no idea what would happen then.

How could he warn Bates?

From this distance, Fargo's Colt was useless. He could get his bullets close enough to pin the rifle man down but hitting him would require sheer luck. And Fargo was too much of a realist to depend on luck.

Again the question nagged him—how could he warn Harold Bates?

11

An hour earlier, Rafferty had untied Callie Bates and let her walk around the small cabin. He sat at the table sipping whiskey and pulling on jerky and keeping his gun aimed directly at her. It took her a while to get her legs. The circulation had been cut off for so long, she moved like a little old lady afflicted with a bad case of arthritis. He finally relented and walked her outside so that she could pee in some privacy on the far side of a jack pine in the fading light.

For her part, she was still agitated from all the thinking she'd done while tied up. She'd reviewed her life and found that she felt pretty miserable about nearly every aspect of it. Too many men, too many confidence games. But worst of all was her relationship with her father. He hadn't exactly been a sterling character but he'd been loving, if nothing else. She'd never known who her mother was. Her father said that she'd died in childbirth. He was always vague on the subject. They'd gotten along well until she became a young woman and began to make a living much the way he did. That was the part she didn't understand. He'd wanted her, he'd told her angrily one night, to be a lady. And that now she wasn't any better than her mother had been (it was the last time he'd ever mention the woman to her) nor any better than he himself was. He'd sent her to a private girls' school, clothed her in the latest fashions, and even sent her East for extended stays so that she could learn culture firsthand.

But somehow, he'd continued to rant, she'd turned out to be a criminal just like her old man. Then, to her astonishment, he'd slowly collapsed into a chair and begun to cry in the unwilling and difficult way a man cries. He said that he never wanted to see her again. Three days later, she'd made plans with Branson and Devol to double-cross him when the robbery was finished.

She'd heard from him only one more time. A letter had reached her from his prison. He'd said that he couldn't find it in himself to forgive her but that he nonetheless had asked a priest to say a mass for her once a month, that she might straighten up and become a lady after all. He had enclosed a holy card of the Madonna with a prayer on the back. The card was crude, hand drawn, not pretty like those mass-produced on fancy presses. On the back was an address: Munoz, Texas. His letter added that he'd spent a week there and had found peace. Shortly after, he was captured.

When she was finished peeing, she pulled up her britches and stood for a long moment beneath the clean brilliance of the stars. She would never make sense, not even to herself. She longed to be friends with her father. When morning came she'd leave this part of the country and head for civilization.

"Get over here," Rafferty snapped. "We're going to tie you up again."

She said a nasty word.

"Just to a chair this time. Not all bound up."

"Gee," she said, "you're a refined gentleman after all. And here I thought you were just another thug."

"Somebody's going to slap that mouth of yours shut for good someday, Callie."

"Yeah, and it'll take a real man to do it. Which sort of lets you out, doesn't it, Rafferty?"

He walked over and started to slap her, but she ducked under the blow and laughed at him.

But she paid for it.

Rafferty hit her full force in the stomach. She sank to her knees and then collapsed flat on the ground.

She couldn't ever remember being hit this hard before by anyone. The pain was so singular, so fierce, that she couldn't imagine ever feeling right again.

To make things even worse, Rafferty knelt next to her. His right hand cupped her breast, feeling for the nipple. She resented the fact that even though she despised him, even though she quite literally wanted to kill him, he was expert enough to make her nipple harden and then stand erect.

Someday, she would make him pay for all this. Someday.

Harold Bates was afraid he was going to wet his pants as he shuffled down the narrow corridor that led to the prison yard.

Usually when he went outside, he was happy. The combination of solitude and nature always nourished him, made him able to deal with one more day in this hellhole.

But not tonight. There was just this dread he had.

He opened the door carefully and peeked out.

The dusty vast yard was silvered with moonlight. The buildings were cast in deep shadow. He could hear the lonely sounds of the men settling in for the night. If things went right, he wouldn't ever have to hear them again.

He stepped out into the prison yard, worrying a little about what was to come.

He decided he was being foolish. Skye Fargo sure as hell knew what he was doing. He'd probably busted men out of prison before. His reputation was such that he could do virtually anything he put serious effort into.

Bates turned now to the front gate. It looked a long, lonesome distance away. But it was time and he'd better start walking.

Fargo would be there waiting for him.

Fargo jumped from the lowest branch of the jack pine and then headed for the gate and the guard. His plan had changed. He wasn't going to sneak up on the guard now. That would take too long. Fargo was in a race with that shooter up on the porch. He just wished he knew what the shooter had in mind. Maybe he was going to shoot Bates, or perhaps he'd learned that Fargo would be helping Bates and planned to kill the Trailsman.

It took Fargo a full frantic minute to find the size and shape of rock he needed. He stood in the shadows of the trees, right on the edge where he could easily be seen. He had no choice. The guard was just now turning, military style, to walk away from the gate, his back to Fargo. The guard would walk to the end of the wall and then come back to the gate. This was his patrol.

Fargo hefted the rock a final time. If he missed, the guard would be alerted and open fire. And when he opened fire, the entire prison would come awake. Getting Harold Bates out would then become just about impossible. It would give the shooter plenty of time to do what he'd planned to do all along.

Fargo raised his throwing arm, took aim, and let fly.

The bank bag sat in the middle of the wood table in the two rooms the old priest thought of as his rectory. He was a humble man and so the poverty of his surroundings did not bother him.

Tonight he had much graver problems than the shabbiness of his living quarters. He had counted the money in the bank bag—the money that was the fragile lifeline of this entire town—and he had come to realize that he had even less money than he'd thought. He'd been handing out cash during his time here without really keeping track of the money that was left.

How would he help his flock when the money was gone? They would still need medicine and clothing and sometimes shelter and food. And there would be emergencies; poor people always had an emergency. Indeed, when you were poor, the simplest need sometimes became a matter of life and death.

But where was the money to come from?

He was old, and he held no sway with the bishop. It was the one thing he'd always resented about his beloved church. Church life was no different from secular life in that regard. There were important priests and unimportant priests. The important priests not only got the choice assignments, they also got donations from wealthy contributors.

The world was not fair. In his younger years, this thought would have ignited rage in the old priest, but he was too weary now to do anything but sigh sadly and gaze at the nearly empty bank sack.

What was he going to do?

The rock didn't knock the guard unconscious but it struck hard enough to disorient him for thirty seconds, during which time Fargo raced across the wide dusty patch of earth. He dove into the man with such force that the guard's rifle was knocked from his hands and slammed into the ground. Fargo followed this up with three strong punches to the man's head.

Fargo ripped the guard's key chain from his belt loop and then lunged to the gate, jamming the key at the lock but missing on the first attempt. It took three tries before he was able to successfully slot the key. The guard was moaning. He wouldn't be out for much longer.

Fargo got the gate open and lurched inside. Shadows clung to the inside walls. He ran to them in a zigzag fashion, in case the shooter decided to open up on him.

He crouched low, moving along the wall to get within shooting range of the porch. And then he got his first glimpse of Bates.

Bates looked frozen in place, no more than five feet from the door he'd just walked out of. Maybe Bates had told the warden about the break and all this was a setup to trap Fargo. Then the quiet night inside the prison walls broke into a warlike cacophony of rifle and revolver fire. Just before the first slugs began to rip into the wall behind him, Fargo saw yellow flame bloom from the shooter's rifle and saw Bates take a bullet in the leg. Only later, on reflection, would the Trailsman think how strange it was that with such a clear shot the rifleman would opt for shooting Bates in the leg. Why not kill him? Skye Fargo would realize that the shooter had to have his own secret reason for simply wounding the aging bank robber.

But now there was no time to think. Now there was only time to throw himself away from the wall and start rolling on the ground in the direction of the gate. From here he could see that it had not been locked as yet. Since the guard had been moaning already, it wouldn't take much longer for the man to get on his feet again and block Fargo's escape.

The bullets came so close to his face that he was momentarily blinded by dust and sand, and a shot nicked off a piece of his bootheel.

Shouts, increased gunfire—everything was crazy. When he finally got close enough to the gate to stand up and make his run for it, he saw the guard appear as if by magic.

The guard carefully sighted his rifle. It was clearly going

to be a pleasure to burst Fargo's head like a ripe summer melon. A guard did not often get to have such an honor.

He made one mistake. In taking the time to sight well, he gave Fargo an opportunity to raise his Colt. Fargo had nothing against the man personally so when he fired it was simply to blast the carbine from the man's hand.

There was something comic about the moment—the guard preparing to fire and then throwing his weapon up in the air as Fargo's bullet ripped across his knuckles. The guard screamed in a high-pitched voice and then sank to his knees. He probably wasn't even in all that much pain. He'd just been shocked by Fargo's surprise move.

Fargo fired twice more above the collapsed man's head so that the guard wouldn't try to stop him as he came hurtling through the open gate.

The gunfire had not lessened in volume or fury—if anything, it seemed that even more people were firing at his back.

Fortunately for Fargo, he'd cleared the gate and was now running full speed toward his Ovaro stallion.

12

Rafferty had heard him coming and was waiting in front of the cabin door with a carbine pointed straight at the Trailsman. Fargo ground-tied his horse and walked up to the man.

"Where's Bates?"

"Somebody figured out what was going on. Or somebody told Grieves what was going to happen tonight. They were waiting for me."

Rafferty swore several times then held out his hand. "Your gun."

Fargo shook his head. "I want the girl. Then we're riding out."

Rafferty spat out a stream of chewing tobacco. "The girl? You didn't get Bates. That was the bargain."

"Right now, Bates is probably in the infirmary." He told Rafferty everything that had happened at the prison.

"Grieves," Rafferty said.

"He set it up."

"Sure sounds that way. And who else would it be?"

"How'd he find out?" Fargo said.

Rafferty didn't answer. There was a long silence. Fargo gazed up at the stars and the silhouettes of the pines against the moon-painted sky. The air was fresh. Fargo wanted to be far away from here as soon as he dealt with Rafferty. He hadn't forgotten his grudge and never would until the debt was settled.

"Come in the cabin."

"I just want the girl."

"We need to think."

"About what?"

"About how I'm going to find that money without Bates helpin' me. Now get inside, Fargo."

Callie was lashed to a chair. This time she wasn't gagged, and her restraints weren't tight enough to cut off her circulation.

"How's my father?" she asked before Fargo had time to even get completely inside the cabin.

"I thought you didn't care about him," Fargo said.

"I've been thinking about him. I guess we sort of let each other down. We were both to blame."

This was the gentlest he'd seen her. He liked her this way. For once her attitude matched her pretty face.

"He got shot but he should be all right," Fargo said. He gave her a quick account of the failed prison break and her father being shot in the leg.

"He'll never get out now," she said, sounding forlorn. Her eyes hinted at tears about to fall, but then she sat up straight in the chair and took a deep breath. Fargo was impressed with her self-control. This was a scrappy young woman. It would take a lot to break her and if she got half a chance she'd break you instead. And with no regrets.

Fargo went over to her, bent down, and started untying her.

"Thanks, Fargo," she said. "I've changed my mind about you. You're not nearly as much of a stupid saddle tramp as I thought."

"I guess that's about the finest compliment I've had in years," he said, not sparing the sarcasm.

Rafferty had apparently been so lost to his thoughts that he hadn't realized what was going on right in front of him. He raised his carbine. "What the hell you think you're doing?"

"I try and break Bates out," Fargo said, continuing to untie her, "and you let the girl go free."

"But you didn't break him out."

"That wasn't my fault."

"So you two just walk out of here?"

"That's about right," Fargo said. "We just walk right out of here." Fargo glanced up at him. "This is about the worst square knot I've ever seen."

"I'm real sorry," Rafferty said. "Next time I'll try and do better."

"Square knots aren't that tough," Callie said. "But I wouldn't use them to tie people up. There are a lot better knots for that."

"Shut the hell up, Callie," Rafferty said.

"I'm so damned sick of you," Callie said.

Fargo kept untying her.

"I thought I told you to stop untying her," Rafferty said.

"I guess I didn't hear you," Fargo said.

"I could kill you right now," Rafferty said, taking aim.

Fargo's Colt appeared with magical speed. He eased up to full height.

A classic face off. They were within a few feet of each other. Both men would die in any kind of shoot-out, and they knew it.

So did Callie.

She leaned over and undid the rope around her ankles and then stood up. "I need to pee."

"Shut up, Callie, or you'll get it first," Rafferty snapped.

"Well, this is really stupid," Callie said. "You two standing here facing off." She nodded to the door. "Now I'm going outside and take a pee and if you two boys behave yourselves, I'll tell you where the money is."

"You really think you know?" Rafferty said, sounding almost ridiculously excited.

"Yes, Rafferty," she said, as if to a child. "I really think I know. Now if you'll excuse me, gentlemen, I need to pee."

And she sashayed right out the door.

"You sonofabitch," Harold Bates said. He lay on a cot in the prison infirmary. He hated anything that had to do with medicine. Even a whiff of iodine convinced him that death was hovering near.

"It's just a leg wound. Quit bitching, Harold," Warden Grieves said.

"You ever hear of gangrene?"

"You won't get gangrene. We got a doc comin' out from town."

"Prob'ly not a real doc."

Grieves rolled his eyes, then said, "We need to talk, Harold."

They were the only two people in the infirmary. Grieves had made sure the door was closed and the windows shut tight. He made a fist and punched Bates on the right thigh, right in the middle of the wound then clamped his hand hard across Bates's mouth. The outlaw bit him hard on the palm.

Now it was Grieves's turn to shout, "You sonofabitch!"

Harold Bates moaned. He held his leg with great tenderness and rolled back and forth on the cot, biting his lip as the pain kept getting worse.

For his part, Grieves stood there and shook his hand, making damned sure that Bates hadn't broken the skin. He should have punched the bastard was what he should have done. Soon as Bates bit him, he should have done it.

A few more minutes passed in silence as each man dealt with his wound. Only now were the guards able to restore order in the prison. All the gunfire had excited and spooked the inmates. A situation like that could create a riot. The guards earned their keep on a night like this. They clubbed any man at will who tried to keep the tension going.

Bates said, "I still won't tell you."

"Oh, Harold," Grieves said, affecting a sorrowful voice. "You're not built for torture. I could've punched you in that wound of yours a lot harder. And you could barely take it. Think of all the other things I could do to you. You might not even live through them."

"Yeah, but at least you wouldn't have my money. I'd have the satisfaction of that, anyway."

"Up in heaven you mean? Is that the kind of satisfaction you want? Seems to me it wouldn't do you much good up there. If you want satisfaction, seems like you'd want it down here."

"You sure got a line of bullshit, Grieves."

Grieves took a stogie from the breast pocket of his suit coat and lit it by thumbing a lucifer afire. He took a massive hit on the cigar, inhaling the heavy gray smoke as deeply as he could. Next to a piece of ass, smoking a cigar was the finest time a man could have. Actually, given some of the dogs Grieves had slept with, a cigar was frequently better than a woman.

Grieves knew Harold liked cigars. Rafferty could pick them up in town, but he couldn't pick up cigars as good as these. Same for whiskey. A man could buy all the whiskey he wanted in town, but he couldn't buy the kind of whiskey Grieves drank. That took special ordering from long distances.

"I only want half of it, Harold."

"Yeah, well you ain't getting any of it. How's that for ya?"

This time he didn't punch the wound. He thumb fired another lucifer and pushed the flame right on the rawest part of the wound, the entry point.

People in Chicago could probably hear the scream Bates gave out.

"I told you, Harold. I warned you fair and square. Now there may be some men who can hold up to torture but I'm not one of them and neither are you. And I'm a hell of a lot tougher than you are, Harold. But punching a wound like that—or putting a flame to it—Harold, sooner or later you're going to give up and tell me. So why don't you save yourself a lot of grief and just get it over with. Tell me right now and right here."

"Screw yourself," Bates said manfully, but tears from the pain were slithering down his sallow cheeks.

When Grieves smashed his fist into Bates's wound, Harold told him everything he wanted to know.

Rafferty took no chances. He stood in the cabin door and watched while Callie went behind the largest of the scrub pines and did her business.

She walked back toward him, hitching up her jeans. "You didn't have to worry about me running away, Rafferty. I wouldn't leave Fargo behind. Unlike some other people I could name, he's my friend."

"Shut up about Fargo and tell me about the money."

She walked past him. He followed her like a loyal dog back into the cabin. Fargo sat at the table, rolling a cigarette.

"You got Rafferty here all excited," he said. "And you got me a mite interested, too."

She shrugged. "I don't know why I didn't think of it a long time ago." She paused. "Boy, am I hungry."

"We were talking about the money," Rafferty said.

"I talk better when I've had something to eat."

Rafferty stalked over to where some jerky lay on top of

a box. It was wrapped in a piece of newspaper. He pitched it to her.

"You sure know the way to a girl's heart, Rafferty."

Fargo laughed, knowing it would irritate Rafferty. "He's a charmer, all right."

"The money," Rafferty said.

She unwrapped the jerky and frowned. "You call this food?"

"The money."

She wrapped the jerky up again and tossed it on to the table. "I'd rather not eat."

"So now you won't tell us?" Rafferty said.

"No, Rafferty. I'll tell you. But I'm making one provision."

"What's that?"

"That the three of us go get it."

"You mean Fargo, too?" Rafferty said.

"Wait a minute, Callie," Fargo said. "I didn't say anything about going."

"If you don't go, he'll kill me, Fargo."

Fargo frowned. "Why the hell you want to tell him, anyway?"

"Because if I don't, he'll just follow us. Then he'll kill us when we find it. This way we'll at least know what he's up to."

"Where the hell is this money, anyway?" Fargo said. "Keeping in mind that I want to be back on the trail."

"You need to have some purpose in life, Fargo," she said. "Maybe being tied up all this time was good for me. I got a lot of thinking done."

Rafferty slammed an angry fist on the table. "Where the hell's the money?"

But Callie wasn't to be hurried. She wanted to share her thoughts with Fargo. "We're a lot alike, Fargo. We just drift around. We don't have any real purpose."

"Just tell me how far away this money is?" Fargo said.

"Now you're starting to sound like him, Fargo. Here I'm trying to tell you something—something about your eternal soul—and all you can think about is that money."

"I just want to know how far out of my way I have to travel," Fargo said.

She smiled at Rafferty, taking pleasure in angering him. "It's not more than forty miles from here. My father told me that in a letter he wrote me some time back."

"Which direction?" Rafferty said.

"That'll have to wait till dawn," she said, "when we leave."

13

Harold Bates woke up just before dawn. At first he couldn't remember much of anything. He'd been running a substantial fever all night and between being sweat-soaked and in some very sharp pain, his sleep had turned into a carnival of freak show attractions. Monsters had pursued him all night long. He'd felt like a child again. A couple of times he even cried out for his mother, something he hadn't done in decades. The only good part of the entire parade of ugly creatures was a brief episode in which his penis had grown to mammoth proportions, a fact noted by a clutch of bosomy women all begging him to touch it. But then the monsters came back and spoiled all his fun.

Roosters and inmates awoke at about the same time. The gathering sounds of pots and pans, various animals, and town workers pouring into the prison for the day quickly reminded him of his situation.

And his situation was simple enough: Grieves had ruined his chance for escape. While Bates hadn't trusted Rafferty or even Fargo, he would at least have had a chance at freedom with them. Now he was not only still in prison, he was also wounded.

Another memory came to him, one so ugly his entire body jolted at the thought of it. Sometime during the night, suffering from fever delirium and the intentional, measured brutality of Grieves's torture, he'd told the warden about the little town where the money was.

He jerked upright. He'd been so damned careful to keep the secret to himself, and then last night—not only was he still in prison, not only was he wounded, now he wouldn't even have his money.

Grieves had left him some tobacco. Bates sat on the edge of the infirmary cot rolling himself a smoke. He didn't care how, but he was going to escape this place and get to the little town and reclaim the money, which was rightfully and indisputably his. He would get a gun, and though he did not consider himself a violent man, he would shoot anybody who took it from him.

He smoked and thought, and then he remembered what day it was—supply day. There would be a wagon from town, one of three such wagons a week. Dutch Prentiss always unloaded the midweek wagon because many of the supplies were for the various tasks done in the barn where he and Bates worked. Barrels were exchanged, full ones for empty ones.

Bates was a small man . . .

. . . and these were very big barrels.

But like a cautionary from the gods, just then pain speared his leg wound with such force that it lifted his bony bottom a half inch off the couch.

Moving around was going to be a bitch. He would have to endure a kind of pain he'd never known before. He wasn't a tough man. He was a bank robber. While others had sullied the calling with violence, he'd seen the whole process as relatively civilized. You needed money more than the bank needed money, so you took it. But this was not necessarily uncivilized. At worst it was merely selfish.

But he knew that his thinking was all crap. Bank robbing was a dangerous job and people on both sides got killed all the time. Many of those who didn't get killed ended up where he was, in prison.

No, he could no longer delude himself. He wasn't a gentleman bank robber. He was a crook, no different from other crooks. And now he was an old and weary crook. His last hope for any kind of life was that money he'd hidden, which meant that his days of forgoing violence were over. He'd kill if he needed to. He had to locate and claim that money no matter what it took.

He sat imagining the empty barrels the wagon always returned to town. He'd have to distract the driver and Dutch some way, pull their attention to something else, and then hurry into one of the barrels.

Then what?

How do I get to the town? How do I find the money? What if somebody in the town already found the money and spent it? Or what if they found the money and turned it over to the bank? Or what if his wound was such that gangrene really did set in? Or what if he was simply too old to make such a trek in his condition?

All these thoughts overwhelmed him, paralyzed him for the moment. He rarely suffered from self-doubt. He set himself a goal and worked toward that goal.

But in his fragile condition now . . .

But then he found his steel. Found his grit. Found his guts.

It was his money. His money. And nobody else was going to get it.

He eased himself off the cot. He put one foot firmly on the floor, and then the second foot. For a blessed moment there, there was no pain. Hell, he was going to be fine. Apparently, the worst of the wound had been sweated out through the night. He could walk; he could travel. He could get his money.

He took a step toward the infirmary door.

Hell, he felt downright strong, downright tough.

By this time tomorrow the money would be his.

That was when he collapsed to the floor, a scream so raw in his throat it felt as if a razor was slashing it . . .

No strength, and no sensation but pain.

He wept. A pain unlike any other he'd ever known raced up his right arm and exploded across his chest. The heart attack endowed him with a single mercy—it killed him in an instant.

This part of Texas had seen some sad times earlier when some otherwise sensible Rio Grande ranchers had decided to go prospecting. Gold tempts all men and these were no different. Wives and children were left behind to work the ranches and farms. Some of the families never reunited.

There were other sad times, too. While some of the Apaches tried to make peace with the white man, not all did, and not all white men wanted peace. There were crazed warriors on both sides.

Finally there was the land itself—fertile to be sure but a victim of sometimes radical shifts in weather that could wipe out the work of an entire season. Just about every-body in the region believed in God—as what sensible person doesn't?—but sometimes His ways were not easy to understand or deal with.

Despite all this, Fargo thought as he rode alongside Callie and Rafferty, the new world here was taking shape. Man was making his mark, bringing early civilization with all its great rewards and frustrating entanglements. Here you'd see a ranch house newly painted, cattle and crops the best. There you'd see a settlement with one or two false fronts gleaming proud in the dusty sunlight. And in many places, you'd see children, the ones who would carry on the work of their parents and grandparents when that time came.

Ordinarily, Fargo would have been in the proper mood to appreciate all he saw. While he didn't believe in constantly braying about his patriotism—and he was damned suspicious of those who did—it kept a silent constant vigil in his heart.

But it was hard to keep that vigil when a cynical, violent man like Rafferty was riding next to you.

The time was ten o'clock. The temperature was in the eighties. They had headed into a desertlike stretch that was mostly slopes and deep gullies. There wasn't much talk, and, for Fargo at least, there was no sense of companionship. He'd come to like Callie but he was sorry that despite the way she'd softened, she was still so intent on getting the money for herself. It was bad money and it would only bring her more grief. She was too young to understand that.

Around noon, they put in at a creek to let the horses drink while they sat in the shade of a shale overhang.

Callie said, "I'm wondering how my father is."

"Shut up about your old man," Rafferty said. "I'm sick of hearing about him."

The few times she'd spoken this morning, the words had all been about her father.

"Like I said, Callie," Fargo said. "It was just a wound in the leg."

"Yes, but things happen. Infections and all."

"I'm sure he's fine." Fargo had no idea if he was fine, of course, but there was nothing else to say. She wanted reassurance, even false reassurance.

"How far you figure we've come?" Rafferty said to Fargo,

drinking from his canteen, silver pebbles of water dribbling down his unshaven jaw.

Fargo shrugged. "Doesn't matter, like I said. You want to hurry but it's too hot to hurry. If Callie's map is right, we won't get there till morning."

"We could ride straight through."

"That's up to you, Rafferty. Me, I like a little sleep. I want to be fresh when we pull in there. We don't know what we'll find."

"What the hell's that supposed to mean?"

Fargo sighed. "What the hell you think it's supposed to mean? Just what I said. None of us has ever been there. We don't know what we're heading into. Maybe it's an outlaw town. Or maybe it's a Mexican town and they don't like whites. Or maybe it's just a sleepy little town and everything'll be fine. But it's not that big so three of us riding in there and starting to snoop around—they'll get suspicious. And when they get suspicious, there could be trouble. That's what it means, Rafferty. And that's all it means. I can't see the future any better than you can."

Callie smiled at Fargo. She liked hearing Rafferty told off. The one chance they'd had to be alone—when Rafferty had gone down to dive into the water to wash up before leaving this morning—she'd confided how scared she was that Rafferty would kill them at some point. Fargo agreed, but didn't say this to her. He said that Rafferty was interested in the money, not in killing them, unless they wouldn't cut him in when they found the money. He didn't believe that, and neither did Callie, but it was another instance of reassuring her with lies.

Rafferty got up and walked down to his horse and mounted up. "You coming or not?" he said. "You two're like old ladies. Won't ride straight through. Got to get your beauty sleep." He snorted and started riding on ahead.

Fargo looked at Callie and said, "Sure you don't want to marry him?"

She laughed. "He'll probably ask you to be his best man."

"That I wouldn't count on."

As they walked down the slope to the water hole, she said, "You know, I never really thought of killing anybody before. Never thought I could do it. But Rafferty—I think maybe I could actually do it. I think I could maybe actually get some real pleasure from it. That's terrible, isn't it?''

"Well, if it is, then I'm terrible, too. I'm going to kill him first time he does anything I don't like.''

She stopped him, and held his sleeve. She looked up into his lake blue eyes. "You really hate him that much?''

"Yeah, I do.''

She studied him even closer. "How many men you think you've killed, Fargo?''

"Not any more than I absolutely had to.''

She shivered a little. "Sometimes you scare me.''

He smiled. "Every once in a while, I scare myself.'' He was only half kidding.

14

Father Michaels had a dream the night before, only to wake up and realize that it had been just that—a dream.

There was a bank bag, and whenever it was nearly empty, all the old priest had to do was leave it on the table overnight and by morning it would be filled up again with money for Father Michaels's poor flock.

Now he chastised himself for such foolishness. Such thoughts were for children. Jack and the Beanstalk. Red Riding Hood. The Cow in The Moon.

He said his mass that morning completely preoccupied with the money. He stumbled over his Latin. One of the altar boys had to whisper a reminder that he had forgotten to bring the chalice down to be filled with water and wine, and at communion he twice tripped over the hem of his robes.

Luckily for him, morning mass was mostly attended by old women. The men and the young women had been up much earlier, starting the day's work. The old women would be forgiving of his absentmindedness.

After mass, he ate a meager breakfast of a biscuit and a cup of coffee. He was just finishing up when a woman came to the kitchen door and said, "Father, it is Ramon. He is shaking again and his eyes are rolling back. We must get him to a hospital." She spoke quickly, terror obscuring some of her words. She played constantly with the ends of the scarf she wore on her graying head. Only one of her brown eyes worked. The other was dead and milky from a childhood accident.

Well, Father Michaels thought, *I knew it wouldn't be long before the very last of the money would be spent. And it'll be spent right now.*

The procedure with Ramon Montez was always the same. The boy would be difficult to look at. All his limbs would be twitching with such ferocity that occasionally a bone would break. Father Michaels had no knowledge of medicine. All he knew was that the eleven-year-old suffered from a rare disease of the central nervous system. When he got this bad off, all they could do was get him to the hospital and let the doctors work against time to try and save his life. The doctors would have to be paid. The aunt would need money so that she could stay in town with the boy however long she was needed.

He pushed himself up from the table, feeling a despair that he knew to be a sin, and told her he would be with her momentarily. She said she would wait for him at the wagon. She said he was the kindest man she had ever known, and began to cry, then turned abruptly away, rushing back to the wagon.

He was near the desk where he'd put the bag last night when he began calculating what Ramon would require. He remembered now what each trip cost, and realized that there wasn't enough money to give the woman.

To make sure that his recollection was correct, he counted the money once again. He had been correct. There was not enough. He would simply have to give her what he had. The hospital was poor. They needed money as badly as the priest's people did.

He walked up to her at the wagon. He could hear the boy. As usual, the lad made a low keening sound, a subdued wail that you sometimes heard with dying animals.

"I'm sorry," he said. "This is all the money I have."

She held her hand out and as he placed the bills in her palm, he glanced into the buckboard. The boy's spasms were so violent that he appeared to be in the throes of some crazed dance. Sweat gave the boy's face a glazed sheen. His eyes were closed. You could see where his teeth had ripped into his lower lip, the blood a vicious red. The stench of urine was strong. The heavy woolen blanket his aunt had put on him lay across his feet. The wail was heartbreaking to the old priest's ears.

He reached down to take the blanket and place it over

the boy again when the sun caught the gleam of the ruby in his ring. He realized that there was a way to pay the hospital after all.

He loved the ring, of course. He took a pride in it he occasionally confessed as a venial sin. It was the only thing he did take pride in.

But what was an old man's pride compared to the health of this boy and others in the town?

The aunt watched with dark somber eyes as the priest worked the ring off his finger. His joints were arthritic and so the ring did not come off easily.

When she realized the implication of what he was doing—he was going to give her his ring!—she said, "Oh no, Father. Your ring has powers that protect us all."

He smiled. Working hard at twisting the ring over his swollen joint. "I love good tales, too. But no, God has the power, not this ring. Now you take this and give it to the doctor at the hospital and tell him it is worth a lot of money. This will pay for future trips to the hospital for everybody in the town."

"Oh, Father—" she started to protest.

"There we are," the priest said, finally managing to slide the ring off and set it in her hand atop the money. "Now you take this and hurry to the hospital."

As if to emphasize the urgency of the moment, the boy let out with his loudest wail yet. The aunt put her hand to her face as she peered into the buckboard afraid he'd taken a dramatic turn for the worse.

The priest hurried her to the front of the vehicle and boosted her up on the seat. She took the reins in her hands and turned back to the priest. "Bless you, Father."

"Hurry now. Hurry."

He stood standing in the dust her quick departure left hanging in the air. When he reached down to touch his ring—a habit of many years—he smiled.

She had done him a favor. She had taken away the last vestige of his vanity.

The sun was no friend. By noon the temperature had reached ninety-four. Rafferty rode ahead of them, like an outrider. Fargo was glad to be shut of him. It gave him a chance to talk to Callie.

"You could always turn that money back to the bank," he said.

She grinned. "I never thought of you as a preacher, Fargo."

"The story'll get out. Somebody found the money. They'll put a price on your head and every bounty hunter in this part of Texas'll be after you."

"That's if Rafferty doesn't kill us first."

"I'd worry more about the law than I would Rafferty."

"He told me he isn't afraid of you. He said you're all reputation and not much else."

"Everybody's entitled to his own opinion."

"That doesn't make you mad?"

"You managed to change the subject. Like I wouldn't notice."

"Aw, Fargo. Don't preach at me. I hate that. The fact is I don't know what I'll do when I get my hands on that money. Maybe I will give it back to the bank."

"But then again, maybe you won't."

The grin—she had a good one. Sweet-girl clean and sexy-girl seductive, both at the same time. No easy task. "But then again, maybe I won't. You mean even if I was to offer you three or four thousand, you wouldn't take it."

"Nope."

"How come?"

"Jinxed."

"Jinxed? What's jinxed?"

"The money's jinxed. People dead because of it, man in the bank and Devol and Branson killed in cold blood. Your old man in prison. And Rafferty off his skull because of it. Sure sounds jinxed to me."

"Rafferty was off his skull before he ever heard about this money."

"Maybe so. But that doesn't make any difference to Devol and Branson."

She shuddered. "God, you're bringing it back." She was obviously recalling seeing two men—living, breathing men, with lives and history and kin that loved them—shot dead without hesitation right in front of her. "He'd kill us the same way, wouldn't he?"

"Sure would."

They rode on in silence for a time.

"I guess you're right, Fargo."

"How's that?"

"What you said about it being jinxed. It sure has made a whole lot of people crazy."

"Including you."

She laughed. "That's right. Including me."

Fargo's own laugh was cut short by the two rifle shots that missed the brim of his hat by no more than an inch.

"Hit the ground!" he shouted.

She wasted no time. She landed on the dusty trail only seconds after Fargo did. The bullets continued, ripping up dirt, rock, cactus. She followed him in rolling behind the only boulder he could find. It wasn't sufficient but it was the best he could do.

They waited until the shooter needed to reload.

"We weren't paying attention," he said.

"To what?"

"To Rafferty."

"It's Rafferty shooting at us?"

"Sure. He's apparently decided he doesn't need you after all. He knows where the town is and he can find it all by himself."

"I don't think I've ever met anybody like him. He's a really evil man."

Fargo smiled at her. "You mean you just figured that out? He killed two men right in front of you."

"Yeah, but he didn't try to kill me."

"That's because he wanted sex and then he wanted you to get him to the money."

"Oh yeah, I guess that's right."

He was almost irritated by her naivete. She hadn't believed Rafferty was evil until he was evil directly to her. There were people like her everywhere. You could warn them about certain folks and they'd never listen until those folks turned on them personally. By then, at least usually, it was way too late.

Rafferty had reloaded. The air was alive again with the sound of bullets tearing into everything around them.

Callie put her head down and piled her hands on top of her head. Between bullets, she could be heard muttering prayers in a nervous little girl voice.

Fargo knew he had to get to his horse and get his Henry or Rafferty was bound to kill them sooner than later.

He had just started to pull himself carefully into an upright position when he heard Callie cry out. He glanced at her and saw her hand clutched to her shoulder in disbelief. It gleamed with the thick red blood of a fresh wound.

15

When Rafferty heard Callie cry out, he eased himself to his feet, crouched low and headed for his horse. From here, it was impossible to tell how badly he'd wounded Callie. But that didn't matter. He'd wanted to get a head start on them and now he had one. Fargo and the girl would be tending to her wound.

He rode hard. He formulated plan after plan as his horse took him closer and closer to the town. The problem with plans, he knew, was that they rarely worked out. You always found yourself, at the last minute, having to alter the plan or dismissing it altogether.

He knew only one thing for sure. The first thing he needed to do was find a white man who had lived in the town for longer than a few years. A man who might remember when Harold Bates had spent some time in the town. That would be a starting point. Later he would have to deal with Fargo again.

He reached the town when the scorching heat was at its worst. The place was about what he expected, a dusty, dead collection of adobe huts with a large adobe Catholic church in the middle. The only living things on the streets in this heat were a few children, a few chickens, a few cats, and a few dogs. The streets reeked with horse turds of various sizes. Apparently the sight and smell of all this horse manure didn't bother what passed for the leaders of this small sad place.

There was one fancy building. This had been the courthouse. The town had once been the county seat, but the county seat had moved on up the line. All the windows in the courthouse were smashed now and dirty words were scribbled on its exterior walls. The other example of vanished importance was the cobblestone street that ran three blocks down the center of the town.

The jail, such as it was, was just another adobe building with a big SHERIFF painted in black above the doorway. The only difference between it and the other five or six commercial buildings was that all its windows were barred. In back there was a crude gallows but Rafferty figured that was for show. The government wanted to do its own hanging these days, legal and proper, no vigilantes needed.

Rafferty reined in, tied up at a wobbly hitching post, and walked over to the door. He wasn't surprised to find that the door didn't fit quite square with its frame and that a man had to push hard to open it. This went right along with everything else in this town.

What he walked into was a war memorial, or something very like it.

One wall was covered by swords, rifles, and pistols as well as the dress uniform jacket of a Union officer. It was a fine and fancy jacket, too fancy perhaps. He imagined that the enlisted men had snickered when they saw their West Point captain strutting about in something like that. He'd been in the army, too, and he'd had no time for the peacocks and popinjays who seemed to have gotten into the Indian wars not to press the white man's way of life but so they could dress up and play war. He'd seen a suffocating amount of death, had held boys no older than fourteen dying in his arms while he'd whispered the lies and reassurances that they were going to be just fine, just fine.

He had to admit that the man in the photographs, peacock or no, looked like a pretty tough man. He might be fifteen pounds overweight but between the long scar on the right side of his face and maybe the angriest pair of dark eyes Rafferty had ever seen, the man sure looked formidable. The photographs showed him in front of a company of men, talking to a general in front of a commander's tent, aboard a mythic-looking white steed, and standing barechested over the man he'd just knocked to the ground during the course of a bare-knuckled boxing match.

Quite a history, Rafferty thought. His eyes shifted to the man with his feet up on the desk. Buried in all that lard was the man in the photographs. The years had not been merely unkind to him, the years had been merciless. He was not only grossly fat, he even had some kind of sickening red rash on his neck. He wore a black patch over one eye. Some men looked dramatic with such a patch. The obese lawman just looked even more unsightly and strange. Then there was the smell. Apparently bathing was not something the town required of their lawman. The odor was so sharp that Rafferty caught his breath. He realized the smell was somehow medicinal, not just regular old dirt and grime. The only comic aspect of all this was the snoring. If the bastard kept it up, the whole building would probably collapse on him, he was making so much noise. Rafferty was surprised the bars on the windows weren't jittering under the assault of noise. What sort of fallen human wretch was this, anyway?

Rafferty half shouted, "Wake up!"

Clyde Culhane brought up a six-shooter just before opening his one good eye and said, "Way ahead of you, mister. Playing possum's a good way to trap folks." He smiled with tiny blackened teeth. "Pretty bad smell, huh?" He kept the six-shooter trained right on Rafferty's heart.

"What the hell is it?"

"Some kind of salve the doc gave me for this rash I got."

Rafferty's skin began to itch. He wondered if he could pick up the rash just standing near this foul creature.

It wasn't much of a wound but there was blood and pain, and that was enough to send Callie into a ten minute stretch of panic. What she needed more than anything was to be calmed down, something Fargo managed to do while he showed her that the bullet had only torn a piece of flesh from the top of her shoulder and then passed right on by. He cleaned it as best he could. Next came the piece of cotton he'd torn from the clean shirt in his saddlebag. The wound was near the juncture of the shoulder and arm so he ran the cotton over the shoulder and then down under her arm. She wouldn't be able to move it quickly without loosening it so he suggested that when they started riding, that she use just her left arm to hold the reins.

Even though she protested, he said that what he wanted her to do was rest for a while before they resumed their trip. She told him how tough she was and he said that tough was good and tough was fine but tough had yet to put color back into her chalk-white cheeks or the gleam back in her blue blue eyes. He quoted an old doc he knew who said that half the pain of any gunshot or knife wound was the shock of getting it. The mind as much as the body.

Fargo carried her over to the shade of a few stunted pines and laid her down on the blanket he'd brought along. He let her sip from his canteen. She said again that she was tough and would never go to sleep now and he said that was fine and understandable but that was about all he got said because she was sound asleep before he even had time to finish rolling himself a smoke.

"So you're just passin' through," the lawman named Culhane said. He'd taken his feet off the desk and was now sitting up straight. Now if he could only do something about the stark acrid smell of the salve, and the ungodly look of his rash, which looked like nothing so much as squirming maggots feeding on fresh meat.

"That's right, just passin' through."

"Far piece out of the way to be passin' through."

"I must've got lost."

Culhane smiled. "Every once in a while somebody gets 'lost' and comes through here looking for that money."

"What money would that be?"

Culhane smiled with those blackened tiny baby teeth. "You trying to shit a shitter, mister?"

"The name's Rafferty and I don't know what you're talkin' about."

"Of course you don't. You're 'lost' is all."

"That's right."

Culhane picked up a pocket knife and began to dig out the dirt beneath his nails. "Town's so dusty, man is filthy half the time."

"Uh-huh." Rafferty looked around. "Well, I just wanted to let you know I was here. And would be stayin' for a day or so."

"Well, I'd be happy to give you the directions you need, mister. Won't be much for you to do around here." The grotesque man was having himself a merry old time. His blue eyes twinkled like Santa Claus's on Christmas Eve.

"You got a saloon?"

"Yessir, right down the street."

"You got any kind of hotel?"

"Nossir, that we don't have. But we do have a whorehouse where they'll let you stay overnight if you pay them a little extra."

Rafferty smiled. "That don't sound too bad."

The lawman laughed. "You might not say that after you've seen those gals. They ain't exactly beauties. And a couple of 'em are fatter than I am."

Fat, Rafferty could abide. Just as long as they didn't have anything remotely like the lawman's rash. "Well, I always introduce myself to the lawman when I hit a town."

"That's right nice of you."

Rafferty touched the brim of his sweated-out tan hat. "Maybe I'll see you again." He turned and walked back to the door.

"Should tell you one more thing, mister."

Rafferty half turned and said, "What would that be, Sheriff?"

"They don't much like gringos here."

"That's no surprise."

"That means they wouldn't tell you where that money is and they don't. I been here long enough to know that wherever it was hid, it was hid so well that nobody's ever come close to findin' it. Not even me."

"Now you're getting me interested, Sheriff. All this talk about this money—"

The man stood up. He was even larger than Rafferty had guessed. But on his feet, all that bulk was imposing. He could move a lot faster and a lot more deftly than Rafferty had imagined. The mean look he wore was a lot more impressive than his badge. Rafferty realized then that he was brighter and cagier than he seemed. Rafferty would have to watch himself.

"Just one warning, mister. They're my people. They don't like me much and I can't say that I like them much better. But they're honest people and they don't hardly ever cause me any trouble and so I protect them. Anybody threatens them or hurts them, I kill them. I backshoot most of the time but if the man does something that really riles the people up, I let 'em use that old gallows out back. They like that gallows. They turn the whole thing into a festival.

111

Name it after some saint whose name I can't ever remember. The saint of justice, they say. I've never seen these folks happier than when they're hanging somebody. It makes them feel important and I can understand that. These folks don't have much in the way of material things but by God they have their own ways of justice." He smiled with those terrible teeth. "I just thought I'd better let you know that, mister."

"I appreciate that, Sheriff. I'll try real hard not to get myself hanged. How's that?"

This time the lawman didn't smile. "That's entirely up to you, mister. Entirely up to you."

They were riding again by midafternoon. Callie probably didn't feel as good as she claimed she did but Fargo was happy to see her put up a good front.

They didn't ride hard. They'd agreed to make camp tonight and ride into the town in the morning. Fargo had brought it up, saying that was what he wanted to do. She wasn't up to riding any faster than they were right now.

She said, "You'd be there by sundown if it wasn't for me."

"Not unless this horse of mine sprouted wings."

"I'm slowing you down."

"No you're not. And shut up about it."

She gave him the famous Callie grin. "Now you sound like Rafferty."

"Thanks. He's my idol."

"I kinda thought he might be."

More silence. More riding. The few times Callie did talk for the rest of the day, she spoke of her father and not the money. Funny how people could deny their own feelings. When he'd first met her, she'd convinced him that her father meant nothing to her, that she in fact disliked and distrusted him. But then he went and got himself wounded—and not wounded all that badly from what Fargo had been able to see—and then she started worrying about him, wondering if she hadn't been wrong about him. She started thinking maybe they should see each other again, and hoping that there would be some way they could patch things up.

The Rio Grande rolled on. Birds and dogs along the river

112

started making those lonely sounds that sundown always brings. Or maybe the birds and the dogs didn't sound different at all, Fargo thought. Maybe the melancholy you heard was just in the human ear. Maybe it was the person's own melancholy that he heard.

By the time they put in for the night, Callie was dozing off in her saddle. She looked little-girl sweet, fighting sleep. Fargo helped her down from her horse and then started gathering wood for the fire. It was getting a little cooler, and they were hungry and tired. He took her roll and laid it out for her and then helped get her set up for some serious sleep.

Fargo smoked and gnawed on some jerky and drank coffee. He figured that if a lawman ever needed a way to torture a prisoner within the bounds of the law, all he'd have to do is get Fargo to make him a pot of coffee. His stuff was so bad you could get a confession from somebody in under three minutes.

A quarter moon appeared with golden grace just as voices on a small boat could be heard on the nearby river. He wondered where they were going. Maybe some place exciting, maybe some place he'd never been. He had a boy's keen sense of adventure. Wanderlust was both his blessing and his curse. He wanted to see and do everything he could before he finally settled down at some distant date in the future.

He laid his head back against his saddle, slipping his hat down over his face. He could use some of that sleep himself.

He was just dozing off when he felt a small but sure hand glide over the crotch of his jeans. He was instantly alert. As were certain other parts of his body.

Callie slid his hat off his face and moved herself up his body so that her mouth could find his. He came fully alive when her tongue stabbed inside his lips. By this time, her deft little hand had unbuttoned his crotch and she was stroking the head of his long and rigid shaft.

Then he was returning the favor. He moved his hands over her shirt, brushing against her full breasts, while he began to unbutton her blouse. Soon his tongue was lapping and kissing her nipples into eager, chewy rose-colored nubs.

He leaned her backward, toward the fire, and stripped

her britches off. They were both in great need of satisfaction and so they moved on each other recklessly, furiously, him parting her legs and using his rod to dive deep inside the wet hot juicy cleft of her sex.

He wriggled his hands under her buttocks so that he could lift her, grind her into him, so that he could feel the moisture sliding from inside her down across the perfect pale globes of her bottom. For her part, her cunning little fingers urged him on by grabbing his manhood every chance she got, doubling the blinding pleasure he felt, hurrying him toward what they both hoped would be a mutually timed climax. Their only hindrance was her flesh wound, which they had to be careful of.

They changed positions twice, him taking her from the back so that he could thrust lustily at her from a fresh angle, and her rolling on her side, putting a leg over his shoulder so that he could penetrate her even more intimately than before. And then after a time they fell back to their original position, him on top. He was now riding her with dizzying force and speed, his own wails mixed with hers.

Deeper and deeper, harder and harder, they drove until their shared need exploded in lunging bodies, cries that rivaled those of wolves and coyotes, and enough shuddering joy to satisfy a dozen lesser lovers.

They lay naked in the firelight, their skin a reddish-gold, their sweat dried quickly by the cool night wind off the eternal rolling river.

"I do believe," she said, "that that was the best time I've ever had in the romance department."

"I would have to say the same thing."

"Oh, sure. All the women you've had."

"Quantity doesn't equal quality."

" 'Generous of spirit,' as our old parson used to say. That's you."

"Skye Fargo, sage and saint. That's me."

"Don't forget to add 'master lover.' "

"I'm too modest to say anything like that."

She laughed. "You getting a little chilly? I am. I don't want to ruin this by waking up with pneumonia."

"That would sort of take the fun out of everything."

They sat up and got dressed and then sat by the diminished fire, drinking coffee and trying to warm up.

"It's a good thing you're such a great lover, Skye."

"Oh, why's that?"

"Because if I had to judge you by your coffee—"

She slid her good arm around his shoulder and said, "I wonder what my father's doing right now."

She was silent for a time. He knew she was thinking about her old man. The sadness was upon her again.

"I just have this real bad feeling, Skye."

"Most of the time those real bad feelings don't come true."

"That he'll die before we can patch things up."

"He's one tough bird, Callie."

"But not like he used to be. He kinda wore out somewhere along the line. I could see it even before that last robbery. He always bragged that this kind of life was easy street. But it wasn't. He always had to watch his back. You know, with the law. And that takes its toll on a person."

"Yeah," Fargo said, thinking of the times he'd been on the run from the law. "Yeah, it sure does."

She put her head on his shoulder. A few minutes later, she was snoring. He lifted her up, carried her to her bedroll and gently settled her in for the night.

Rafferty knew that the fat sheriff was tracking him, but by nine o'clock that night, he didn't give a damn. He was in the only saloon in the whole place and had enough whiskey in him not to give a damn about anything.

Sheriff Culhane knew his people, anyway. Rafferty must have talked to twenty Mexicans since the time he'd ridden in here and not a one of them would cooperate with him. None of them spoke English—or they pretended not to, anyway—they just shrugged when he asked them about the money. In front of him, they showed fear. But after he left and they talked among themselves, they were all giggles and smiles. The dumb gringo, their laughter said. The dumb gringo thinks we will help him. The dumb gringo will never find the money.

He had wanted to talk to the priest but the housekeeper said that he was not feeling well and was down for the night. He wondered if she was lying. He was sure he'd seen her with one of the small knots of people who were laughing at him.

Now, as he drank, he was convinced that the priest would know. A little place like this, filled with Catholics who went regularly to confession, a priest knew everything.

He smiled to himself as he glanced around the saloon. The reason nobody had found the money, he reasoned with the perfect clarity of the drunkard, was that nobody had ever thought of going to the priest. Yes, that was it. Fools had come after the money and no wonder they hadn't found it. Rafferty was no fool. He was a man of sophistication.

He glanced around the saloon. The place smelled like a latrine. The drinkers were Mexicans. The bartender looked like a half-breed. Only now did Rafferty begin to feel uncomfortable. He was the only white man in the place.

He heard a laugh and whipped around knowing instinctively that the laugh was about him. He scowled at the men laughing. They stopped the moment they saw the anger on his face. They dropped their eyes, afraid.

Anger took him. Images of the things he'd like to do became vivid in his mind. How about walking over to that card table where the laughers were and killing every one of them? He was fast enough with his gun to do just that. Or how about taking the kerosene lantern at the end of the bar and hurling it against the back wall. The rotted wood in this place would catch fire in seconds. Or how about grabbing the saloon girl over there and have her service him right here at gunpoint? She was a Mex. They'd hate to see one of their own girls—even if she was a whore—touch a white man like that, even if she was forced to.

But then his head cleared. It was as if he'd been caught up in some fever dream, fueled with rage. He was calm again, purposeful.

The priest. Yes. In the morning. And no housekeeper dodge about him being too sick to talk. He'd talk all right. He'd see that Rafferty was not a man to fool with. He'd talk plenty. A priest didn't intimidate Rafferty any more than anybody else did.

A lightness in the head, a heaviness in the body told

Rafferty that he'd reached his liquor limit for the night. He needed to be clearheaded and purposeful in the morning. He needed to focus.

The bartender started to reach for the whiskey bottle but Rafferty held up a halting hand. The bartender shrugged. Set the bottle back on the shelf.

Was that a smirk on the bartender's feminine mouth? Rafferty should grab him and beat the man right in front of all his Mexican cronies.

For a terrible moment, he felt helpless, as if he'd wakened to a nightmare. How had a white man come to be standing in the midst of all these Mexes? Maybe he was dead and this was hell, all these Mexes.

Steady now, he thought, as he turned and all the eyes at all the tables began to watch his exit.

And then he stumbled.

Damned board was loose and he tripped over it. It wasn't as if he was going to fall all the way to the floor. He didn't lose his balance that badly. But he stumbled all the same.

The whole place went up in laughter.

The stupid gringo. The clumsy gringo. Thinks he's so tough. Stupid gringo.

Then, unaware that he was doing it, he pulled his gun out and fired three times into the ceiling and shouted at the laughers, "You think it's funny, you dirty Mexes? You think it's funny?"

They might be Mexes but that did not mean they were dumb. They could easily see that this man, for whatever reason, had been pushed to his limit and was now not only drunk but a bit crazy, too.

He glared at them for a long moment, going from brown frightened face to brown frightened face, and then he turned and made his careful way to the batwings.

When he was halfway down the dusty dark street, they started laughing again. He imagined that they laughed all night.

In the dawning light, Fargo could see that the wound had drained more out of Callie than he'd expected it would. The stiff and arduous way she moved down to the creek told him that. She stripped off her shirt and washed herself off. He would have enjoyed watching her wash her breasts a lot more if she didn't look so pained while doing it. He worried now that maybe the wound had gotten infected, that maybe poison was moving through her body. Maybe there would be a doc in town.

He made coffee and gave her all of the lone biscuit. Usually he would have divided it in halves. She sat on a large rock with her legs crossed at the ankles. He'd asked her several times how she was feeling. She managed, in a false chirping voice, to say just fine, even though her complexion and the dullness of her eyes said otherwise. He admired her courage. She wanted to get to her father. She wanted to make amends before one or both of them died. And she obviously wasn't going to let anything—not even a little poisoning from a bullet—stop her.

The trouble came when she tried to pitch herself up on her horse. She heaved upward all right but somehow her hand didn't grab the saddle horn with enough force and she slid right back down, collapsing on the hard, sandy earth.

He ran over to her and helped her up. This close, he could see how bad her eyes were. He put the back of his hand to her forehead. He wasn't good at guessing how high a fever was but this one was plenty hot and plenty high. "We need to get you to a doc."

"C'mon, Skye. I'm fine."

"Sure you are, Callie. That's why you can barely stand up. We were going to ride hard to get to town fast. But we're going to take it nice and slow and when we get there the first thing we're going to do is find you a doc."

"I'll be fine."

He knew there was no use arguing with her, so he didn't bother. He helped her back up into the saddle.

"Maybe all that lovemaking we did last night wore me out," she said, making a frail little joke.

"I have a hunch it was lead poisoning that wore you out."

"And here I was trying to compliment you."

She was clearly hoping that her banter would convince him that she was feeling fine, and that there wasn't any good reason to waste time looking for a doc. Again, Fargo didn't bother to argue.

They set off.

Fargo spent a lot of time trying to figure out what Rafferty was doing. Once again, he was struck by how everybody had lost their minds where this money was concerned. He'd been around enough gold and silver strikes to see what fools and monsters men became when they thought there was great wealth at stake. Having a little money was fine. He liked the free enterprise system that the politicians were always touting. But great wealth—that was another matter.

Half hour into the ride, she pitched head first off her horse, falling into a grassy patch of ground that he hoped absorbed some of her fall.

He grabbed his canteen. When he got her rolled over on her back, he saw that she'd cut her head. The gash was maybe an inch long and lay across the center of her forehead. He tilted her head so that she could drink from the canteen. The skin felt hotter than it had before. Her eyes fluttered open but for at least a minute they didn't seem to comprehend anything. She drank but much of it dribbled right back down the right side of her mouth.

"You remember what happened?"

"Huh?"

"You fell off your horse."

"Oh."

"You're going to ride with me."

"Oh."

No expression in either her voice or eyes. He wasn't a medical man, but the state she was in sure didn't look good to him.

It took him some time to struggle her up into his saddle and then hold her in place while he climbed on himself. He took his own reins with his right hand, letting Callie lean against his arm, and with his left he took the reins of her horse, letting the big bay follow.

Right now, the town seemed very far away. He tried not to think about anything crazier happening, like her getting sick and dying from what had seemed to be nothing more than a damned flesh wound.

They crept on toward town. He couldn't discount the possibility of Rafferty appearing somewhere along the way and bushwhacking them. Rafferty wouldn't want anybody to keep him from the money he now considered to be his own.

But it was difficult—impossible—to keep his hand near his Colt when he had to keep one hand on Callie and the other on the reins of her horse. He just wished somebody would burn all that damned money. It had brought nothing but bad luck.

Warden Grieves left just after dawn. He had a Derringer up his sleeve, a Navy Colt in his holster, and a Winchester in his scabbard. He had a fresh mount, dried fruit and nuts for his travels, and a canteen of water cold as a witch's tit flopping against the ribs of his animal.

He had also brought a map, field glasses, leather gloves. He traveled in the sincere belief that by nightfall—with any luck—he would be a very rich man.

16

Rafferty didn't have the best of mornings. Not only did the dusty brown people of the town not help him, they were downright mocking. Not even the men, who should have been especially afraid of him, feared smirking or laughing or spitting on the ground as they told him that he was not only a fool but that he was not wanted here.

The place smelled of heat and goat shit and food that curdled his stomach. He stomped up and down the so-called streets that were little more than feet-worn paths, sneering and snarling and hoping to scare up some coopera-tion. But something had happened and now Rafferty's real-ity was beginning to feel like a bad dream. Where was the fear, the terror he usually inspired? My God, what was wrong with these people?

At one point, he got so desperate he stood in the central street and fired his gun three times into the air.

They stood under the shadowy overhangs of the few busi-ness establishments, standing there in sombreros and sera-pes and ignorant brown stares—they stood and watched him and didn't run. Even now, even with the firing of his gun, many of them grinned and joked among themselves.

Didn't they realize how easy it would be for him to just start shooting them down, as if they were pieces in a shoot-ing gallery? Ten, twelve men could be killed in a few minutes.

The only real response he got was Sheriff Culhane wad-dling up the street. He didn't even have his gun drawn. When he reached Rafferty, red-faced and sweaty, he said, "I warned ya, Rafferty. Kinda drives people crazy when they come here lookin' for that money. These folks ain't about to cooperate. So you might as well save your bullets."

"All they need is a little slappin' around."

Culhane shook his fat head. "Wouldn't recommend that, Rafferty. Fella come through here—Chichester was his name—and he slapped quite a few of 'em around." He nodded back toward his office. "That gallows back there?"

"Yeah? What about it?"

"They ganged up on him and dragged him back there and hanged him."

"And you didn't stop them? You're supposed to be the sheriff."

"I was over to the saloon. My night to play pinochle with the boys."

"You didn't hear 'em lynching a man?"

"How the hell could I hear them? There were only six, seven of them. They musta been pretty quiet about it. Because I sure didn't hear 'em. I s'pose it was that player piano. I always tell Jake—he's the owner over there, Jake Foster—I always tell him he keeps that damned piano too loud but he never does listen to me."

If he'd been in a good mood, Rafferty would have been laughing out loud. Standing before him now was the laziest, most incompetent lawman he'd ever spoken to. Culhane was a joke. Rafferty would have had a tale to tell every saloon denizen he encountered the rest of his life.

Instead of laughing, Rafferty just smirked. "You mean they try and lynch me, you probably won't hear them?"

"That's a possibility. Tonight's my pinochle night, in fact. And I never miss my pinochle night."

"How about turnin' down the player piano?"

"Well," the lawman said, "I ain't had no luck with Jake. Maybe you should talk to him."

The two men locked gazes. Rafferty saw that beneath the blubber and the bullshit, beneath that carefully contrived mask of stupidity and indifference, there was cunning and guile and intelligence. Culhane had probably been part of the lynch mob himself.

Rafferty said, "Where's the church?"

"Well, I reckon that'd be the only building with a cross on top of it." He smiled. "You gonna confess your sins, are you, Mr. Rafferty? That might take a long time. That's a mighty old priest. You just might wear him out."

Now it was Culhane's turn to smirk.

"That's the thing about our little place here, Mr. Rafferty. Bandits and gunnies and assassins of every stripe come through here from time to time and they don't find it very hospitable. And they don't like the way all the people make fun of them with their eyes. There's a kind of contempt, I guess you'd say, in their eyes. And the bandits and the gunnies and the assassins always try and scare the people. And some of the people they do. I reckon every place you stop you find people who're afraid of everything. But that wouldn't be most of the people live here. Because they know that this place is gonna go on. When all the bandits and gunnies and assassins are planted in the ground with maggots eatin' out their innards, this little place'll be standin' right here, and life goin' on just as always."

Rafferty, badly needing to beat on somebody, brought his arm back and made a fist that could dent steel.

But the lawman, who seemed to have put on a pair of testicles when he left his office and came waddling up here—the lawman just grinned and said, "I been punched by a lot tougher men than you, Mr. Rafferty. And I'm just like our little town here. I'm still standin'."

The grin went. The guile and intelligence came back to the eyes. Now it was joined by cold blue malice. "You take care of yourself, Mr. Rafferty."

And then he waddled away.

By the time they reached town, Fargo had to grip Callie tighter to keep her from falling off the Ovaro stallion. She had begun to have fever dreams. Several times she muttered things to her father and, once, she began to cry.

The town was curiously quiet for noonday. The heat was in the eighties. Maybe that was why there was so little activity but Fargo doubted it. Something else was going on.

On the front of an adobe home that was small even by local standards Fargo found a sign that said DOCTER. He hoped that whoever had put up the sign could doc better than he could spell.

Fargo eased himself down from his horse, taking Callie with

him. She was in and out of consciousness now. He tried to stand her on her feet but that lasted for only one step. He swept her up and carried her to the door, his boots crunching on dried dog turds. DOCTER was not a master of cleanliness, either. But this was the only medical place he'd been able to find.

He kicked at the door. Nobody answered.

He stood in the heat, which was still climbing. It would likely hit ninety-five by midafternoon.

The door opened and a small, white bald man with viciously red blood smeared all over his hands appeared. His white shirt and blue trousers were also soaked with blood. "Help you folks?"

"She was shot. She's got a bad infection."

"Well, bring her in."

A dusty stream of sunlight painted everything a scruffy gold. There were two straight-back wooden chairs, a small desk littered with a sprawl of papers and books, and three glassed-in cabinets for medical instruments and medicines. Fargo didn't see any diploma.

An operating table stood in the center of the house's only room. Across the surface of the table was a line of cats, squirrels, possums, and raccoons. They'd all been pretty well carved up. One possum had had its eyes removed and stared at Fargo with empty, bloody sockets. There was a pile of tails from assorted beasts.

"I'm just practicing," the old man explained in his doddering voice. "You know, since the trouble?"

"I guess I don't know what you're talking about. The trouble?"

The old man smiled and looked ten years younger. "You don't? You're not from around here?"

"Afraid not."

"Well then," the doc said, "in that case we'll get right to work."

His expression showed great relief.

The trouble—Fargo wondered what the hell he was talking about.

The doc bundled up all the cadavers in the stained sheet on which they rested, carried them to the door, and flung the whole mess outside.

He came back in and begin to take medical instruments from a glass cabinet. Fargo was just about to ask the doc if he didn't want to wash up first when the doc took a pint of alcohol from the cabinet, upended the bottle in the palm of his left hand, and proceeded to spend two full minutes scrubbing up. Better than nothing.

During this time, Fargo gently lowered Callie to the operating table then slipped her shirt off. She had awfully nice breasts and when the doc saw them, his intake of breath articulated eloquently that old age hadn't completely driven sex from his mind.

"She's a looker."

"Yes, she is."

"Wife?"

"Friend."

The old fart giggled. "Wish I had a 'friend' like that."

Then he went over her and examined the wounded area. "She's infected, all right."

"She going to be all right?"

"Most likely. But I don't like to make predictions. That's how I got in trouble." He continued to examine her as he spoke. Every once in a while, his right hand would come very near to brushing her left breast. Fargo couldn't blame him there. The doc looked up. "I'll need an hour or so."

"I'll look around town."

The doc laughed high and sharp again. "You do that, son. But I need to warn you, there ain't twenty minutes of 'lookin' in the whole place. You'll be back here in no time."

Fargo went to the door and stopped. He turned back to the doc. "You mentioned 'trouble' a couple of times. What sort of 'trouble' did you get in?"

The old man looked sad. "I took off the wrong arm."

"On a patient?"

"Uh-huh. They said I was drunk but I wasn't. I had a few but that's a long way from drunk. Anyway, I'm not sure what happened. Soon as I sawed away that arm and laid it next to the man on the table here—I knew I was in deep trouble. I knew I'd taken the wrong arm off. His family didn't understand. I don't s'pose I would either, taking off the wrong arm like that. Long story short, I don't get the business the way I used to. Not since that arm story got around." He shook his bald head. You could see the bones in the top of his skull. There were even liver spots up there. "So people are leery of me. Even the folks I used to give credit to—even the Mexes, who I always thought were my friends. They take themselves and their families up the road apiece. Very good hospital and docs." A sad old man yellow-toothed smile: "I guess the docs over there don't take off the wrong arm."

"I'm going to be damned mad if anything happens to her."

"You think you might kill me?" the old man said.

"Maybe."

"A part of me wouldn't mind. Between the wife dyin' and this arm business—I just don't have the old enthusiasm I had. So if you were to kill me, maybe I'd be better off."

"I don't go around killing people I don't need to, doctor. All I want you to do is make sure that infection doesn't kill her. You should be able to handle that."

"Yep," the old man said just before Fargo left, "I sure should be."

Rafferty had watched as Fargo went into the DOCTER's and now he watched as Fargo left. He'd been expecting Fargo to show up but despite the expectation his mood darkened as he watched the man start walking toward the center of town and the cobblestone streets.

Rafferty stood in the shadowed doorway of a small barn made of mesquite wood. He'd seen the owner leading two horses to a line of date palms where two suited businessmen waited with cigars and impatience beneath the glossy fronds of the elegant trees. He moved back, deeper into shadow, until he was sure that Fargo was well on his way.

The barn had six stalls for horses and a small smithy setup. Colorful prints of Mexican heroes were nailed to various parts of the walls. There was a mythic quality to the depictions. Most of the men held handguns and wore tight, dramatic clothes. Each print bore a name. Mex stuff—he hated it.

The church was less than a block away. Rafferty hurried to it now.

He knocked twice on the rear door of what appeared to be the rectory. While waiting, he tried to smooth himself out a little, tugging his shirt down, taking his hat off and slicking back his hair, preparing himself for a large and cordial smile. He wished he'd taken the time to shave and apply a little bay rum.

The woman who answered the door carried a wicker basket on her fat arm. Her stout white form spoke of inordinate self-confidence, just the kind of woman Rafferty hated most. Nobody could be harder to deal with than a steely-eyed middle-aged harpy like this one.

"Good morning, ma'am." He held his hat meekly in two hands, a lonely wayfarer in the vale of tears.

She wasted no time. "If you're here to see the father, he's asleep. He takes a nap every morning. He needs it and deserves it. I'm going to buy some food. You'll have to stop back later."

He wanted to slap her. She was not only obstinate. She was arrogant. "What time will he be getting up, ma'am? I'm afraid this is an emergency."

She seemed to see him for the first time. Her eyes assessed him up and down. Disapproval narrowed her gray gaze. "You don't go to church here, do you?"

"No, ma'am. I'm sort of a traveling man." Trying to sound like a harmless hayseed.

"And your emergency would be what, exactly?"

"Something I can only tell the father, ma'am."

"Confession then, is it?"

"Yes, ma'am, confession."

She sighed. She didn't seem any more sympathetic—in fact, she most likely saw that he was lying—but she had to be dutiful. This was, after all, a rectory, where all God's children had to be treated fairly—if grumpily. "He just now got to sleep."

"I see."

"So give him at least forty-five minutes and then come back. I'll be back here myself by then."

"Yes, ma'am. I appreciate it."

His humble words were starting to taste bitter in his mouth. He was sick of bowing and scraping to this bitch. But what choice did he have?

Not that he was going to do what she said, of course. He'd walk away and then watch her from the barn. When she was gone, he'd sneak back in here and wake the priest up by making noise.

"I'll be back then, ma'am. And thank you for your help."

She didn't say good-bye, only nodded.

He set off to the barn.

Inside the wooden structure, he walked to the open rear door. The owner was still out by the palms with the two men. They were looking over the horses he was obviously trying to sell them. The men were white and even from here, just by the way they stood, Rafferty could tell that they felt superior to the smaller man, the Mex.

Even though the woman had said she was going shopping, she didn't appear for another five minutes. By then Rafferty was bored and irritated. What was holding the bitch up? He didn't want Fargo visiting the priest before he did. He consciously put Fargo out of his mind for now. He had to concentrate on getting in to see the priest.

Finally, the rectory woman appeared. She walked out into the furious sunlight. She moved quickly for such a barrel-shaped woman.

Rafferty made his own move. In moments, he was back at the rectory. He found the door unlocked and went inside. The taint of cheap altar wine and recently fried meat lay on the still hot air.

Rafferty could hear the priest snoring. He just followed the sound.

The old man slept in the bottoms of his union suit and no shirt. Easy to see he'd been a strapping, hard man many years earlier. He was so pale now he looked like a corpse lying on the narrow white cot in the tiny room. The surprise was that the thick gnarled hair on his chest was still ginger colored. The only thing on the wall was a huge crucifix that depicted a sorrowful Christ who seemed shrunken beneath the large crown of thorns. Rafferty was no longer religious but he was still superstitious. The Christ figure was so imposing, he crossed himself.

He took out his six-shooter, crossed to the cot, jammed the tip of the barrel into the priest's forehead and said, "Padre, you've got one minute to tell me where that hundred thousand dollars is. Otherwise, they'll be planting you in the ground tomorrow. You understand me?"

The old priest struggled to wake up. When his eyes focused, he gaped at Rafferty as if he were an apparition and not a real person. "Who are you?" the priest said. There was no doubt of his fear.

Rafferty smiled. "I'm the devil, padre. Lucifer himself."

17

Fargo wasn't sure what he expected the local sheriff to look like but whatever it was, the size, shape, and general demeanor of the walruslike middle-aged man surprised him.

"Well, well," Sheriff Culhane said, feet up on his desk, fat black cigar between two of his surprisingly dainty fingers. "Mr. Skye Fargo himself. Sure have heard a lot about you." There was a hint of disappointment in his voice.

Fargo smiled. "I'm not seven foot three and I don't have an eye in the back of my head and I'm not the toughest looking man you've ever seen."

Culhane smiled in return. "Yes, something like that. You hear so many stories about a man—you expect him to make the earth shake when he walks."

"Afraid that's not me," Fargo said. His glance around the office told him that Culhane didn't put any more effort into the appearance of his office than he did his person.

"So how can I help you, Mr. Fargo?"

"I'm looking for a man named Rafferty."

For the first time, Culhane seemed to have some dim interest in what was going on in his office. The feet came down, the posture straightened out, the small hand lifted a cup of steaming coffee. He hadn't offered Fargo any. He said, "Oh yes, our Mr. Rafferty."

"So he's here?"

"If you mean is he in town, yes. Exactly where, I couldn't tell you. But I wouldn't be surprised if he was at the rectory."

Fargo said, "You going to tell me he got religion all of a sudden?"

"No," Culhane said, rolling the cigar around in his fingers. "Seems everybody who comes here looking for the money ends up at the rectory. They figure that if the old priest hears confessions, then he just might know where that hundred thousand dollars is buried."

"Does he know?"

"Not as far as I know."

"He cooperative at all?"

The lawman shrugged. "He's cooperative as far as his so-called 'flock' is concerned. I'll give him that much. He takes care of his own. He's a sincere man."

"But you don't think he knows where the money is hidden?"

The lawman shook his head. "Don't think so."

"You know where the money is, Sheriff?"

Culhane let go a loud echoing laugh. "Now just think a minute, Mr. Fargo. You're obviously an intelligent man. Do you think that if I knew where that money is, I'd still be here in this town."

"I suppose not."

"If you've got a family, it's a good place to settle. But if you don't—" He shrugged. "If I had the money, I'd be so far away from here, you wouldn't believe it."

Fargo rolled a cigarette. "You have any reason to arrest him?"

"Not so far. Why?"

"Because it'd make things easier for me."

"I'm afraid that's not my job, Mr. Fargo. Making things easier for you."

Fargo thumbed flame to a lucifer and raised the flickering flame to his smoke. "I'm going after him."

"Be my guest."

"You don't want to know why I'm going after him?"

The lawman smiled with ugly little teeth. "The more I know, the more likely it is I'll get in trouble. And I'd sure hate to be in trouble with Mr. Rafferty. He's a pretty crazy cuss."

"So you won't try and stop me from bringing him in."

"That'll be entirely up to you, Mr. Fargo."

"You mind if I borrow a pair of your handcuffs?"

"There's a pair right over there, Mr. Fargo. Help yourself."

Fargo walked over and took the cuffs from their peg. His feet were loud on the wooden floor. The old lawman watched him but showed no real interest. "I'd hate to have to bet on you two."

"You would, huh?"

"Pretty evenly matched, you two. But I'd give Mr. Rafferty a slight edge."

"Yeah, and why's that?"

He tapped his skull. "Because he doesn't know he's crazy. And that's a blessing. He can really let himself go without being inhibited. Take my word for it, Mr. Fargo. That's a real weapon. When you're so crazy you don't know you're crazy. Doesn't matter to him what he has to do to get what he wants—he'll do it."

"But you didn't arrest him."

"For what? He hasn't done anything yet. What would I book him for, Mr. Fargo? So far he hasn't broken any laws. He just asked me a whole passel of questions is all. And I couldn't answer him any better than I can answer you. I don't know where that money is and I don't care where that money is. That amount of cash always brings out the worst in people, Mr. Fargo. In case you hadn't noticed, I mean."

"Saw the church right down the street. And you think he's there?"

"I wouldn't guarantee it. But from everything he said, that's sure where I'd start looking."

Fargo touched the brim of his hat in a mock salute and said, "Guess I should go pay my respects to the old priest. He might be able to help me. Especially if I promise to help him get some extra money for his flock." Fargo walked to the door. "I appreciate your time, Sheriff."

"My pleasure." He smiled. "Now I can tell everybody I met the Trailsman."

"Remember, I'm over seven feet tall and have three arms."

"I'll be tellin' that to the boys at the pinochle game tonight. 'Seven and a half feet tall, he was. And a gun for every one of his three hands.'"

"And you know the worst thing?" Fargo smiled. "They'll probably believe you."

"Amen to that," the portly sheriff chuckled. "They generally believe anything I tell them."

"What do you want?" Father Michaels said.

Rafferty had let him pull on his cassock and sit in a chair. He drank tepid water from a smudged glass. They were still in the tiny bedroom. A large spider was crawling across the mussed bed. The bedclothes smelled sweaty and hot.

"Now you think about it real good, Padre. Why would a man like me come to this little hellhole?"

The old priest made a disgusted face. "Oh, Lord. It never ends."

"What never ends?"

"You. And people like you. Why don't you spend your time serving the Lord instead of coming here for that money?"

Rafferty put one of his bootheels up against the wall and leaned back. "Good for you, Padre. Now we don't have to waste time. You know why I'm here."

"You look Irish to me. Are you Irish?"

"What the hell's that got to do with anything?"

Father Michaels fixed him with his eyes. "If you're Irish, you're probably Catholic, and if you're Catholic you have to know that what you're doing is a mortal sin."

"The money?"

"The money and treating a priest this way."

"Gee, Padre, you've got me scared now. Guess I'll have to mount up and ride out of here."

"That's what you should do but you won't. You'll be like the rest of them. You'll waste my time until you realize that there isn't any money left."

Rafferty had been expecting the priest to tell him there was no money, that the money was a myth. Instead, he'd startled Rafferty by admitting there had been money but it was gone. "What's that supposed to mean?"

The old priest sighed. "I've never admitted this to anybody before you, but I spent all the money myself."

"You're lying."

The prelate shook his head. "It's all gone. I gave it to the people here as they needed it. I don't know what'll happen to them now. They needed that money. I like to think that God saw that it was left here for our uses. These are poor people."

Rafferty's bootheel scraped down the wall. He stood erect. "I hope for your sake you're lying."

"Freeze."

The voice surprised him. He looked to the rounded open doorway. The housekeeper said, "Hand your gun to Father Michaels. Then step back and put your hands up."

The stout woman handled the shotgun comfortably—he had no doubt she could use it. Even with his own gun already drawn, he knew it was likely that she would kill him.

Still, he hesitated. It wasn't right, some ugly old lady like this getting the drop on him. It just wasn't right at all.

"If you think I won't kill you, you're wrong. It'd be my pleasure. I'm sick of all you scum coming here for that money."

She raised the shotgun so that it pointed right at his head. He turned and sneered, but then he walked over to the priest and handed him the gun.

The priest accepted the weapon and said, "I wasn't lying to you. The money is all spent."

"He isn't lying," the woman said. "He didn't know that I figured it out—that he was using the money to help the people. But where else would the money have come from? He's as poor as the other people here. It came from a satchel behind the tabernacle. But now it's gone. All spent."

Rafferty was so angry at what he heard that he lunged for the woman, not caring if he died or not. He grabbed the barrel of the shotgun. The discharge was deafening and he recoiled two feet back from it. She'd meant to shoot him but the shot had instead torn an apple-sized hole in the adobe wall. She started to raise the shotgun again. He punched her with such force that she collapsed to the floor even before he could tear the weapon from her hand.

He made the mistake of forgetting about the priest sitting behind him. What was some old bastard like that priest going to do, anyway? Even if he did have Rafferty's six-shooter?

The shot from the priest's gun damned near hit him. It seared past his right ear—a hot, momentary sensation that pushed him forward and out of the room when the priest fired off a second round.

With all the gunfire, he had to get out of here. The townsmen were sure to collect around the rectory. They would be happy to shoot him—or maybe let him live momentarily and hang him on the much-used gallows behind the sheriff's office.

He threw furniture out of his way as he rushed out the back door. All that confronted him there was rich but useless farm land. Useless to him anyway.

He needed to get to his horse. No way in this baking heat was he going to leave this town on foot. He would reconnoiter a few miles from here and then sneak back tonight to hunt for the money. He didn't believe that the priest was telling the truth about the money being gone.

He heard people shouting and running now, coming fast to the church and rectory.

He ran down a block of back doors and small loading areas and piled garbage—the rear of the business section. He wished he had his six-shooter. A running man toting a shotgun was sure to attract attention. Between the running and the size of the weapon, they'd know instantly there was trouble.

He forced himself to slow down, to walk as if nothing was wrong. When he found two buildings that offered him enough room to walk between, he headed for the board sidewalk out front. He knew he was sweaty and his upper body was heaving and out of breath.

He just needed to get to his horse . . .

Fargo was walking toward him. Rafferty blinked, not sure that it really was Fargo. But then he knew. And now Fargo had spotted him.

The cobblestone street had become a trap. Rafferty's eyes frantically searched for somewhere to duck into. There couldn't be more than one shell left in the shotgun. Fargo would have at least six bullets.

To his right, across the street, was a saloon. The smell of beer roiled on the hot day. The sedate laughter told him that there were only a few men in there. But they had guns and they would be able to subdue him or kill him at will.

"Rafferty!" Fargo shouted, dropping his gun hand toward his holster.

DOCTER.

The place was within a few steps of Rafferty. It was the only place he could see for shelter.

Fargo fired once, twice, Rafferty escaping only because he suddenly flung himself toward the DOCTER door. He charged it head first as more of Fargo's bullets sought to tear his life from him. He flung the door open inward and ran inside, turning around quickly to shut the door and then turning back to assess what this place had to offer.

Another questionable vision came to him. A young woman sleeping on a white cot. No, impossible. But he blinked and again his eyes reassured him that what he thought he saw . . . was real.

Callie Bates lay asleep on the cot. Beside her the old doctor raised a white head and said, "I'd appreciate it if you'd put that gun away. This is a doctor's office."

"Is there a back door to this place?"

"No."

Rafferty grinned and then ran to the only window, which lay to the right of the front door.

Fargo stood in the street, his Colt dangling from his right hand. Fargo had obviously figured out the situation. He'd brought Callie here and knew she was inside. And he knew the kind of man Rafferty was—one who would kill Callie if he needed to.

Callie mumbled something in her sleep. She sounded like a child.

The doc said, "Who the hell are you, anyway?"

"Doesn't really matter, Doc, long as you do what I tell you to. Because if you don't, I'm going to kill you."

"This is a peaceful town, mister."

Rafferty laughed. "Not anymore it isn't."

The doc sighed, picked up a wash rag sitting next to a basin. "You mind if I do my job? I'd sure hate to get in the way of you killin' people."

"You got some tongue on you for an old bastard."

The doc went about his business. He set the rag down in the basin. When it was good and wet, he wrung it out. Then he laid it with great care and reverence across Callie's forehead.

"Come over here now," Rafferty said.

The doc made a weary face and said, "You'll never get

out of this town alive. Nobody ever has who shot it up. And I reckon from all the noise down the street, you already shot it up some."

"The rectory. Some old bitch with a shotgun." He patted it. "I took it away from her."

"You killed her?" The doc was startled. "She's a good woman."

"Oh yeah," Rafferty said, "a regular saint." He shrugged. "Don't worry. Nobody's dead—yet. And as long as you do what I tell you to, nobody will be dead."

"Except you. Like I said, these people might look stupid to you. But they're not. Most of them are good, hard-working folks who just want a peaceful place to raise their kids up. And they sure don't take to the likes of you."

Rafferty heard his name called. Fargo, of course. He looked out the window. A dusty group of brightly clad Mexicans with rifles had gathered around Fargo. No doubt they were the group that did all the hanging in this place.

"You go out there and tell 'em this, Doc. I'm giving 'em two hours to bring me that hundred thousand dollars. The priest tried to tell me that he'd spent it all. But then I got to thinkin', that's impossible. He didn't spend no hundred thousand dollars just helpin' people around here."

Now the doc was surprised. "You mean that money is really here?"

"That's right. And the priest admitted it."

"I'll be damned," the doc said, momentarily forgetting the situation here. "All these people trekkin' through here, lookin' for that money. I thought it didn't exist. And Father Michaels had it all this time."

"You're not listening to me, Doc. They've got two hours to come up with that money. I want it set right outside this door with two good horses saddled up and ready to go. I'll have the girl with me. You talk to Fargo. He'll know I mean what I say. Anything goes wrong, I'll kill the girl. You understand me?"

The doc just looked at him and shook his head. He said, more wearily than angrily, "There're men like you all over the West. And everyone of you is a fool. You don't think somebody's going to cut you down as soon as you walk out that door?"

"You ask Fargo about me, Doc. He knows I'll kill the

girl. And he knows I'll risk dyin' to get my hands on that money. I want a little somethin' out of this life. And I'm tired of waitin' for it. Now you git on out there and you tell Fargo and that fat-ass sheriff of yours exactly what I want." He glanced at a wall clock. "Two hours. That's all they get. And I'm not going to believe any story about the money bein' all gone, either."

Rafferty grabbed the doc by the sleeve. "Now you get out there and do what I told you to."

The doc nodded sadly. "Let me get just one more look at her. Make sure she's all right. Then I'll go."

"Well, make it fast."

The doc went over to Callie and bent down, checking her vitals carefully. He had positioned himself in such a way that Rafferty couldn't see what he was doing.

Then the doc straightened up and walked with a kind of frayed dignity to the door. He obviously didn't enjoy doing the bidding of a killer.

18

A group of a dozen men stood around Fargo, all of them looking at the house marked DOCTER. They were particularly intent now because the front door had just opened and the familiar face of the doctor appeared. He shouted, "I'm coming out. Don't nobody shoot."

The doc had walked no more than three feet when Fargo heard Rafferty begin piling things up against the inside of the door. He had a weapon and he had a hostage. For now, anyway, he was in charge.

The doc told Fargo what Rafferty had demanded. "Reckon you'd better go talk to Father Michaels. See if that really was all the money."

The townsmen were as surprised as the doc had been about the money actually existing. They had just assumed that the old priest had had a white man's access to money. No white man ever seemed quite as impoverished as a Mexican. The old priest had used bank robbery money to do good things for the town and that only made them admire the priest even more. In a sense, he was a Robin Hood figure—giving to the poor by taking from the greedy. Yes indeed, he was a good man, was Father Michaels.

"He says you know what kind of man he is," the doc said to Fargo.

"Yeah, I do."

"So he'll kill her."

"Yeah, he will."

The doc shook his head. "I never went in for usin' them gallows the way folks around here like to. But if we ever get our hands on Rafferty, I'll personally lead him up them steps and drop the noose around his neck."

The townsmen laughed agreeably at the doc. He was a gentle figure. To hear him this angry, this violent, was amusing. This was the stuff of a good saloon story. It would be told many times over until it bore no relationship whatsoever to the truth. By its final version, it would have doc standing off fifty angry gunmen, triumphing over every one of them. Such is the way of saloon stories.

"He's got us," Fargo said. "There's no alternative."

Sheriff Culhane came next. Fargo described the situation to the lawman. Culhane said, "We could make it easy on ourselves and just rush him."

"Easy for who?" Fargo said. "The girl wouldn't think it was easy when he put a couple of bullets in her head."

"You said there was no alternative. I was just pointing out there was one. I didn't mean we should do it. I don't want that little gal killed either."

"Nice of you," Fargo said. Then he started walking.

"Hey, where you going?"

Fargo didn't answer and kept walking.

He found the priest and the housekeeper in the rectory. The housekeeper had a bad bruise on the left side of her face. The priest sat dazed on a wooden stool. He didn't seem to hear Fargo come in. He just kept staring at nothing.

"I need to talk to the priest."

"He's in no shape to talk."

"Somebody's life depends on it." He explained to her about Rafferty taking Callie as a hostage.

The housekeeper said, "That kind of man, he'd kill her in a minute if he needed to." She walked over to where the priest sat in the tiny bedroom. She leaned over and spoke to him as she would to a child. "Father Michaels, Mr. Fargo is back. He needs to talk to you."

"I should have turned that money over the minute I found it," Father Michaels muttered.

"You did what you thought was right. You helped a lot of good people with that money."

He seemed suddenly alert. He looked up at the housekeeper. "You can't make anything good out of something that is bad. I stole the money just like the bank robbers stole it."

"We'll talk about that later, Father. For now, you need to talk to Mr. Fargo."

She said, "He's weak, Mr. Fargo. Be easy with him."

Fargo nodded. She left the room.

The old priest stared down at the hands he had folded in his lap. "I heard what you said. He'll really kill her?"

"Yes."

"He has lost his way."

"I don't give a damn about his way, Father. I just want to save that girl."

The priest finally raised his head and looked at him. "Yes, of course. But there is no more money and he won't believe that."

"You spent the whole one hundred thousand dollars?"

The pale wrinkled face showed surprise. "One hundred thousand dollars? Oh no, Mr. Fargo. There was only twenty thousand dollars. That was all of it."

"Twenty? But Harold Bates had it all when he came here. He didn't have time to hide it anywhere else."

"That's all there was. A single bag. With twenty thousand dollars in it. And I gave all of it to my people."

"You need to show me where you found the money, Father. And we need to work fast."

The priest shuddered wearily. "But there is no more money. I checked. I'm sure there isn't."

"We need to check again, Father."

Getting the priest to his feet wasn't easy. Fargo had to let him sit down twice before, on a third try, the prelate not only got to his feet but stayed on them. "You'll just be disappointed, Mr. Fargo."

"We have to try, Father," Fargo said. "That's the only thing we can do."

He had to hold the old man's arm all the way and even with that kind of support, the priest's legs were so wobbly Fargo half expected him to just collapse to the ground.

When the doc shouted out to Fargo and started to leave the DOCTER's office, Callie stirred and awoke. She was disoriented at first. It took two full minutes for her memory to make things make sense. The shock came when she recognized the man at the window. He turned once in profile. Rafferty.

She watched as he swiftly crossed the room and began searching through drawers. She wondered what he was looking for so frantically. Did he need medicine? Was he searching for money?

Her question was answered when he found, in one of the desk drawers, a shiny new Colt. Even a medical man had need of a weapon or two in this part of the country. He jammed the gun down the front of his pants and went back to the window. He had leaned the shotgun against the wall. Now he didn't even touch it. He seemed much more comfortable with the Colt.

Half-forgotten words came to her. She'd heard the conversation he'd had with the doc with only a part of her consciousness. Now the words, with full and chilling clarity, came back to her. Hostage. Money. Two hours or the girl will be killed.

She started looking around the bed. If she got up, he'd tie her down in some fashion. She needed something to throw at him. Something heavy enough to knock him out so that she could escape this place. If she got very lucky, she might even be able to get his gun from him.

Gun. There was something she needed to remember about a gun, but she was still disoriented and couldn't quite recall what it was. She knew it was important, though, whatever it was.

She pretended to be asleep but every few minutes she managed to look around the area close to her cot. Boots, a doctor's black bag, newspapers, medicines in an unopened shipping box—nothing that looked useful to her.

She checked Rafferty to make sure he wasn't watching her. He wasn't, and then it came to her. She had an advantage that Rafferty didn't know about, couldn't possibly know. All she needed was a few seconds, and if she was very quiet and if he didn't see her, she might have a chance.

She was just making up her mind to move when Rafferty suddenly—with no warning whatsoever—turned around and found her lying there with her eyes open and one foot already on the floor.

"Well, well," he said, "look who just woke up."

*   *   *

When they first entered the peaceful quiet of the church, the stained-glass windows bleeding beautiful colors across the pews, the only penitent there was an old Mexican woman who sat with a black shawl draped over her head and her large hard knuckles covered with the black beads of her rosary. The priest walked through the stained-glass light of the central aisle, the air sweet with incense from this morning's mass, and in whispers asked the old woman if she would mind leaving, there were serious matters he had to conduct, and he was sorry to shoo her away like this but that she could come back in a few hours. The old woman looked at him with ancient brown eyes and then nodded. Who was she to question the wisdom of Father Michaels, the man who did so much for his people?

Father Michaels led Fargo to the altar. The elderly priest knelt, his knee bones making a cracking sound, and made the sign of the cross. Fargo didn't want to hurry him but Callie was constantly on his mind, as was Rafferty. When the priest was finished kneeling, he struggled to get up. Fargo helped him.

Father Michaels stepped forward to the tabernacle. He opened the small wooden door behind the white silk tabernacle curtain and reached inside. There it was, the solid gold gobletlike container that held the sacred host. Father Michaels reverently carried the piece to the end of the altar where he set it down, crossed himself again, and returned to Fargo.

The priest next lifted the tabernacle itself. It was a single box-shaped piece of oak that had been varnished to a high gloss. The priest carried it down to the end of the altar. This time he didn't bless himself. Only the host—the body and blood of the Christ, as the priest believed—required such reverence.

When he returned to Fargo, he said, "That's where I found the bank bag, Mr. Fargo."

He stepped back, inviting Fargo to take a closer look at the square open space lying beneath the place where the tabernacle had rested. Fargo peered down. A cold and grave-clammy odor came up to him. There was no flooring beneath this part of the altar, just raw earth.

Fargo reached his right arm into the opening. He found

the wooden shelf that the priest had told him about. Empty, of course. "Is this the only opening in the altar, Father?"

"As far as I know."

"You mind if we take everything off the altar so I can look at it?"

Father Michaels looked dismayed. "The altar has been blessed, Mr. Fargo. I don't know if we should—"

"He'll kill her, Father."

"But there's no more money in there. I'm sure of it."

"We have to try everything we can, Father."

Father Michaels sighed. "I'm being selfish, I'm sorry. The girl's life is much more important than the altar. Go ahead and do what you must, Mr. Fargo."

"Thank you, Father."

Fargo carefully removed a large Bible, several candle holders, a number of prayer cards, and the embroidered white cloth that covered the top of the altar. He squatted down and started examining the altar from the floor all the way up to where the tabernacle had been. He found no other opening. The wood pieces had been sawn and varnished with great skill. Each intersection of wood was nailed down tight. No secret compartments; no small openings.

"I'm sorry, Mr. Fargo."

"I'm going to try behind the altar."

The old priest started to say something, most likely that Fargo would find nothing there, either. But he stopped himself. The girl's life was all that mattered. Fargo was right. They had to try everything they could to save her.

There was little light and even less room to work in the space between altar and rear wall. Fargo was surprised when Father Michaels brought him a candle and then lighted it for him. "I want to help, Mr. Fargo."

"I appreciate it."

At first, Fargo thought that the back of the altar was a single piece of varnished wood, but as his fingers began to work along the juncture where altar met floor, he felt a faint draft on his hand. Even more faintly, his nostrils filled with the same gravelike smell he'd gotten from the opening in the tabernacle.

"Father, could you tilt that candle down here so I can see a little better?"

"Of course. Did you find something?"

"I think so," Fargo said.

The single sheet of wood comprised roughly three quarters of the altar's rear section. Fargo could see now that one third of it was of a different piece of wood. Not even the nails matched those of the rest of the altar. The carpentry in the church was nearly perfect, except here, where it showed signs of haste.

"I'll need to take these nails out, Father," Fargo said, indicating the nailheads lined up vertically along the patchwork piece of wood.

The priest nodded somberly. "We have no choice, Mr. Fargo."

"I'm going to need a hammer and a wedge of some kind."

"Of course," the old priest said. He tried to hurry away but his arthritis slowed him down considerably. "Of course," he muttered to himself all the way to the rectory.

Warden Grieves reached town just as the rain started. A bright, hot day had turned without much warning into a gray and wet one. The rain came on with such fury that the trail he rode became mud in only a few minutes.

When he reached the TOWN LIMITS sign, he saw before him a place that looked as if it was right on the cusp of becoming a ghost town. The rain didn't help. Through the shimmering damp curtain the place was pale and dirty.

He didn't give a damn about that now. The thing was to get to the church Harold Bates had finally told him about. Get to the church and get that money.

19

Rafferty said, "You think Fargo's such a big man. Let's see if he comes through for you."

Callie shook her head. "It'd serve all of us right if there wasn't any money. If it really was all gone. That money ruined every one of us." As soon as she finished speaking, he saw her go into a coughing spell that brought out a gleaming glaze of sweat on her face. She was death-pale. Her eyes didn't seem to focus quite right. The wound had left her weaker than he—or she—had realized.

Rafferty, standing at the window, watching the street that was filled with men and their guns, said, "You sound like a preacher."

"Not the life I've led, I don't," Callie said. "I've committed just about every sin there is. And until yesterday, I never thought a thing of it. But yesterday—"

Rafferty tried to pretend—as much for his own sake as for Callie's—that he was in control of the situation. And why shouldn't he be? He had the hostage. He could walk out of here and there wasn't a damned thing they could do about it. If they made one false move, he'd kill her.

But that wasn't going to happen, Rafferty told himself. Fargo would turn up with the money and Rafferty wouldn't have to kill Callie till he was long gone from this town and had lost the inevitable posse that came after him.

Then Mexico. And a life of ease.

That was when Callie said, "Drop your gun, Rafferty. Or I'll kill you right where you stand."

Rafferty was facing away from her, his eyes still on the street. What the hell was she talking about? Why would he drop his gun?

One glance over his shoulder told him that she wasn't faking. She pointed a Colt right at him.

"You didn't watch the old doc very carefully," she said. "He left me his gun."

A picture came to Rafferty—the doc leaning over Callie's cot just before he went outside to talk to Fargo. Rafferty hadn't paid close enough attention. The doc had slipped her a gun.

"Where'd you hide it?" he said, just out of curiosity.

"It was under the blanket at the foot of the cot. You should've watched me a little closer when I was getting up." She gave him a crooked smile. "Now put your gun down or I'll pull the trigger."

He had no doubt she would shoot him. She was that kind of woman.

But then another picture came to him, one he didn't have to imagine. One that gave him some hope.

"I said put your gun down, Rafferty. Right on the floor."

What choice did he have? He put his gun down.

By now, Fargo could see how the money had been hidden. Bates had sawed a fourth of the back of the altar away and had then crawled inside, dug a very deep hole, and dumped the money bags in there.

Because Father Michaels had only been able to see the hole from the vantage point of the opening in the tabernacle, he wasn't aware that there were other bags below the first one. The rake he'd used to fish it out had knocked dirt over the other bags, hiding them from view.

By the time Fargo finished his work, he'd had enough of the damp, gravelike smell. There were three other bags and he handed them out to the priest one at a time. He used a garden trowel the priest had given him. He kept digging just in case there were even more than three.

From time to time, Fargo asked the priest what time it was. Rafferty had given them two hours. They had half an hour to go.

When Fargo finally climbed out from inside the altar, he stood up and stretched his back, his arms, and his legs. It had been cramped in there.

The priest said, "This money rightfully belongs to the bank."

"Right now it belongs to Rafferty, Father."

The priest looked at the stained, once-white bags at his feet. "There has been so much grief over this money. I should've just turned it in when I found it."

"You helped your people."

The priest studied Fargo's eyes. "So you think I did the right thing?"

Fargo shrugged. "That I can't say, Padre. All I know is that you practiced your faith. You helped the poor. That can't be all bad, no matter where the money came from."

"You're kind to say that. I'll never be able to rest easy about it—even if it did all go to the people here."

Fargo put the section of altar back where it belonged. The priest would have to get somebody from the parish to nail it back together. Fargo just wanted Callie to be safe. And then he wanted to ride on. Even his hatred of Rafferty wouldn't keep him around now. He just wanted shut of all this. To ride on. To ride out of trouble.

Fargo took two of the bags and Father Michaels took one. They carried them around the back of the altar and down to the communion rail.

A lone man sat in a pew very near the front of the church. It took Fargo a moment to recognize him, but by then it was too late. The man raised a pistol and pointed it at the priest. There wasn't much Fargo could do. He carried a bag in each hand. Fast as he was, there was no way he could shoot this man before the man shot him.

"You've done my work for me, Fargo," the man said. "I appreciate it."

"You're a long ways from the prison, aren't you, Warden?"

Warden Grieves stood up in the pew. "Yes, but I can see from those bank bags that it was well worth the trouble."

"I take it you know the setup here, Grieves," Fargo said.

"If you mean the girl, Fargo, I don't think I need to worry. I'm sure you and Rafferty can work something out." He looked amused now. "Rafferty's such a sane, easygoing man. I'm sure he'd never think of killing her. Or anybody else. Now you give the priest the bags and have him bring them over to me."

The priest glanced at the bags and then at Fargo. "Nothing but trouble, Mr. Fargo. Nothing but trouble." He glanced down at the three sacks of paper money. They weren't especially heavy. Grieves could cram one each into his saddlebags and then strap one to his saddle horn. They wouldn't slow him down at all.

"Easy now, Padre," Grieves said. "You just bring them over here nice and easy." His gun followed the path of the priest bending down to pick up the bags.

Fargo said, "Give him the money, Father. I don't want you killed for any of this."

"That's very thoughtful of you, Fargo," Grieves said. "You're lucky to have friends like him, Padre."

"He is a good man."

"Sure he is, Padre. We're all God's children, right? Now bring the money over here. And Fargo, if you try anything, you're only going to get him killed. Please keep that in mind. You sure wouldn't want a priest's blood on your hands, would you?"

"Go ahead, Father," Fargo said.

The priest sighed deeply before walking the stretch of floor between himself and Grieves. Much as he had faith in God, he didn't want to die. Few people do.

But, like Fargo, he didn't want the money to go to somebody like the man in front of him, the sneering man with his gun. The priest realized that there was only one hope of keeping the money safe so that the young girl would be released. He didn't know if he was spry or agile enough but he had to try it.

He hefted the bags and saw what he needed to do. But did he have the strength? Was his aim good enough? Was he going to get himself killed and maybe Fargo in the bargain?

He took two steps and then pretended to stumble. Old bones, old muscles brought new pain shooting up his leg, all the way up his arm and into his back.

"What the hell're you doing, Padre?" Grieves said.

Then it was time for the second half of his ruse. The priest had dropped the three bags on the floor in front of him. He pretended to reach out and pick one of them up. He took a deep breath. He needed all his strength, all his accuracy.

He grabbed the bag in his arthritic fingers, lifted it a foot off the ground and then hurled it at Grieves. For the next few seconds, everything seemed to happen in slow motion.

The money bag flew end over end on its course. Grieves, as the priest had hoped, reacted instinctively, without realizing the implications of what he was doing. He jerked his body to the right, so that he could avoid being struck by the money sack. But in doing that, again just as the priest had hoped, Grieves's aim was pulled off Fargo. He fired three times, his bullets searching out the priest. One of the bullets ripped into the old prelate's left leg.

All of this was sufficient to give Fargo a clear and unfettered shot at Grieves. Fargo, being the shot he was, needed only one bullet. His gun roared even louder in this humble house of God.

The bullet took Grieves right in the heart. Blood bloomed quickly on the man's suit coat—the crimson flower of certain death.

His gun dropped to the floor. Even if he'd had any life left in him, he wouldn't have had a weapon to fire. His fingers, coinciding with his last few breaths, clawed at the air as if in search of a trigger to pull.

Then he collapsed and was no more.

Fargo rushed toward the old priest but Father Michaels waved him off. "Don't worry about me, Fargo. Get the girl. Hurry. Time's almost up."

"Now," Callie said to Rafferty, "I want you to walk out the door there with your hands straight up in the air."

Rafferty frowned. "I got in a few fights at the cantina last night. Couple of those boys are standin' out there now. With guns. They don't have real good memories of me."

Watching her stand up had convinced him that she didn't have much strength for anything. He had to lure her close to the door. He had an idea that just might work.

"I open this door, they'll start firing," he said. "They'll kill me for sure."

"No, they won't."

"That's pretty damned easy for you to say. You're not gonna get shot."

"Just put your hands up. You'll be all right."

He sighed. "I'm goin' to prison, missy. I'll probably even

hang. But I'd like to live long enough to see my wife again." He nodded to the door behind him. "I don't want to die in some dusty little hellhole like this."

"You should've thought of that."

"All I'm askin' is for you to walk out right behind me. You can yell to them 'don't.' They'll see you and they'll hold their fire."

She seemed to think it over. He noticed how she had to keep raising the gun she held. Her arm didn't have the strength to hold it up properly. "You try anything— anything at all—I'm putting three bullets into your back. You'll either die or wish you were dead. You understand me?"

"What choice do I have? I try anything and you shoot me. I open the door and the boys in the street shoot me." He was doing some real acting here. He looked as forlorn as he could. "I'm not fakin' it, Callie. I want to see my wife at least once more."

It appeared that she was thinking it over again. Finally, she gave a small nod and started walking weakly toward him. "I've got the gun, remember."

"I ain't likely to forget that."

Then she stood no more than a foot behind him, which was all he needed to open the door half way, put his hands up and say, "Don't shoot, I'm coming out."

There would be a moment of confusion, he knew, on the part of Fargo and the men standing around him. He had counted on that and took advantage of it.

"I'm comin' out now," he said again. He took two steps over the threshold, making sure to pull the door closed behind him, with Callie temporarily behind it.

There had still been no response from the onlookers, including Fargo. They had tempered their desire to shoot the hell out of him. All they could do was wait and see what he did.

What he did was suddenly push the door backward so quickly that Callie was swept back into the office. She managed to fire her gun twice but all the bullets did was rip holes in the wooden door.

Rafferty slammed the door shut and dove for her. She tried getting another shot off at him but he grabbed the barrel of her weapon with enough force to tear it out of her hand. He dropped a punch on her forehead that would have staggered a bull, let alone a winsome little woman like herself.

Rafferty had the gun. He was back in control.

20

Over the course of the next hour, the negotiations went back and forth. What Rafferty wanted was a horse strong and fresh enough to carry himself and Callie at top speed out of town. He wanted all the money stuffed into saddle-bags. He'd kill Callie if he didn't get them.

All this followed the usual pattern. Sheriff Culhane shouted that Rafferty could never go far enough or fast enough to avoid capture. Father Michaels, who looked as if he was very near death, spoke in a weak voice about Rafferty's soul. Fargo just simply put Rafferty on notice that the first time he got the chance, he was going to reduce Rafferty's head to bloody meat.

All this was pretty amusing for the first half hour, the back-and-forth that went on in any hostage situation. But then the same things were said over and over and it got tiresome.

Fargo had seen a number of these situations and they almost always ended the same way. The man holding the hostage got so frustrated with his situation that he forced the law side to kill him. He did this by killing the hostage. Fargo was terrified that this was going to happen here.

He talked to half a dozen men about ways to get into the doctor's place. There was no way other than the front door. He considered setting the house on fire, forcing the two of them out that way. The problem with that was it would still give Rafferty—who would know that he could now never get away—time and opportunity to kill Callie. A couple of the more eager young men came forward and volunteered to rush the front door, making the case that

Rafferty couldn't hold all of them off; however, this was another sure way to get Callie killed.

The only good idea came to Fargo by chance. He'd walked over to where a keg of fresh water had been set out for Culhane and everybody helping him. Fargo was taking his drink when he saw a lone rider coming from the north end of town, the same route he'd taken. A picture came to Fargo of a certain spot about half a mile from the town limits.

He smiled to himself. It just might work. Hell, it had better work. It was the only decent idea he'd had all day.

He went over to Sheriff Culhane and told him what he wanted the lawman to do. Culhane cocked his head back and glared at Fargo. "You haven't thrown in with him, have you?"

"Not hardly."

"So I give him the horse he wants and the money he wants and I just let him ride out of here and nobody tries to stop him."

"That's right."

"And where the hell will you be all this time?"

Then Fargo told him that part of the plan, too.

A smile came to the lawman's face. "Well, I got to say one thing for you, Fargo. You're either a fool or a genius."

"Yeah," Fargo said, returning the smile. "And we're about to find out which it is."

A stretch of hardwood trees lined both sides of the road for a good quarter mile, casting a deep shadow over the stage road and keeping it at least five degrees cooler than the rest of the surrounding area.

Fargo tied his horse in a stretch of timber several hundred yards away from the stage road and moved quickly to the hardwoods. He was a deft climber and proved it by scampering up the stoutest and most heavily foliaged tree he could find.

Now it was a matter of waiting.

Sheriff Culhane had to restrain himself. Every instinct he had as a lawman told him to shoot Rafferty and get it over with. Letting a killer ride off like this was not the right thing to do.

But he knew that if he tried to kill Rafferty and failed—well, Rafferty would kill the girl. Then the Trailsman would come back and take care of Culhane.

All Culhane could do was let his deputy empty the bags of money into the largest pair of saddlebags the general store had and set them on a fresh mount from the livery. He watched—and what a disgraceful thing it was to watch—as Rafferty emerged from Doc's office, one hand tight around the girl's waist, the other hand holding his gun to her head.

Hell, the lawman thought, you could shoot him in the head and there wouldn't be time for him to squeeze off a shot. Not likely, anyway. But there was no guarantee. And since there wasn't, Culhane let things play out the way Fargo wanted them to.

Fargo crouched on the lowest branch he could find. He could part the heavy leaves and see the road. It struck him that a long time had passed. He hoped that Culhane hadn't let any foolish ideas overtake him.

Callie had her whole life ahead of her. Or she damned well better have, anyway.

He just wanted the job over with.

Rafferty took every opportunity to grab some cheap feels from the young woman sitting in front of him. It amazed and amused him that at a time like this, when you were riding as fast and hard as you could given that your animal was carrying two people, your mind could still summon up sexual desire.

He didn't bother looking over his shoulder. Sheriff Culhane would have formed a posse by now and the posse would be riding fast and hard on Rafferty's trail. Rafferty had a surprise in mind. About two miles ahead there was a series of switchbacks that could be useful in confusing any posse, no matter how smart.

He gave in to his curiosity and felt a warning jolt of surprise.

There was absolutely no sight of a posse behind him. Instinct told him there was something very wrong about this. If nothing else, he should have seen dust boiling up from the posse's horses. Maybe Sheriff Culhane was a much wilier man than Rafferty had given him credit for.

Ahead of him was a long run of trees on both sides of the road. He spurred his horse on. He was still thinking about the empty road behind him and why there was no posse in evidence. He was so worried about this that he forgot to cop a feel off Callie. He hadn't copped one for nearly three minutes. For Rafferty, that was a long time.

"I'm damned near ready to put a posse together and go after them," Sheriff Culhane said to the crowd of townsmen in front of him.

A man laughed. "Yeah, and if you mess it up for Fargo, I don't want to be anywhere around."

Culhane had given Fargo his word that he wouldn't tell anybody about Fargo's plan, But he could take only so much criticism from the men. Why aren't we goin' after him? You just gonna let Rafferty get away like this, Sheriff? I feel like goin' after him myself, takin' a young girl like that.

So Culhane had had no choice but to relent and tell them Fargo's plan. Then there was no more talk about going after Rafferty. Nobody wanted to take the chance of displeasing Fargo.

A couple of seconds is all I've got, Fargo said to himself as he saw Rafferty and Callie come boiling toward him on the horse. He squeezed his gun in his hand.

Fargo felt his stomach knot, his bowels go cold and queasy. This had to be executed exactly. He calculated that when the horse's head came below the branch, he had to make his jump. His only chance.

Here came the horse now.

By this time, Rafferty had started looking back over his shoulder with alarm. Something was going on here, something bad. He had good instincts for bad stuff, and bad stuff was afoot.

And that was when the sky came tumbling down.

The collision was not perfect. In fact, the collision was barely a collision at all.

Fargo had hoped to land squarely on Rafferty, so that he could knock the man clean off his horse.

Fargo missed, landing on the rear end of the animal. He damned near slid right off before he could accomplish anything except giving his balls some real punishment.

But he stayed collected enough in that moment to reach out and hook his arm around Rafferty's neck.

Fargo couldn't hold on any more. That was the bad part. The good part was that he was taking Rafferty with him.

The two men hit the dusty trail with the force of a massive steel safe hitting the ground from two stories up. Fargo's gun bounced from his grip. He felt one of his spurs snap off when it angled against the ground.

If either man was hurt, their rage overran any pain. They hurled themselves at each other with the force of grizzlies set on killing each other.

Fargo grabbed Rafferty's gun from its holster and flung it toward the trees. Rafferty unleashed his bowie knife from its scabbard and slashed Fargo across the throat.

Fargo gave into a moment of pure shock. He'd never seen anybody cut a throat from this distance. Rafferty was damned good with that knife. He hadn't hit the jugular but he'd inflicted surprise and a good-sized wound.

The two men started circling each other, Rafferty eager to finish Fargo off with the bloody knife.

Fargo jumped him. It was his turn to inflict surprise. He caught him so unexpectedly and with such force that he slammed Rafferty back into the trees.

He'd hoped that surprising Rafferty this way would knock the knife from the man's hand. But it didn't. Rafferty only redoubled his grip on the knife and then bent down.

Rafferty swept up a rock with ease and hurled it at Fargo. Fargo, moving backward to avoid the rock, stumbled on a small hole in the road. The rock smashed into his forehead, cutting him severely.

He felt consciousness begin to leave him. Cold blackness engulfed him as he tried to force his body to respond in a protective way. He was suddenly too weak, too mentally damaged to get back into control quickly.

Rafferty was on him, grabbing his shoulders and hurling Fargo to the ground. Fargo's vision cleared once again when the back of his head slammed against the road.

It was easy to see what Rafferty had in mind. He was going to finish cutting Fargo's neck.

Spit from Rafferty's mouth dripped into Fargo's face. Rafferty pounded three punches into him. Rafferty wanted him nice and calm for the throat cutting.

Then Fargo saw it, three, maybe four feet away. If he could only crawl over to it. He vaguely wondered where Callie was. Had she just ridden away with all the money in those saddlebags? Had the temptation been too much for her?

Fargo grabbed Rafferty's wrists. For the next few minutes, the men struggled, wrestled, Fargo always moving toward the one thing that could help him now. He knew he couldn't hold Rafferty off much longer. Even Fargo's strength had only so much capacity. He'd been able to push Rafferty away each time he had come for his throat. But not for much longer—

It was close now—close enough to reach out and grab. He had to keep Rafferty distracted. He began jostling his body right and left, trying to buck Rafferty off. All the time ready to make his grab.

But was there time?

Rafferty twisted Fargo's right wrist, keeping his fist at bay. Then, still dripping spit like a wild dog, Rafferty leaned over to slash Fargo's throat the right way. The final way.

A second later, it was Rafferty who cried out. Fargo's hand had found the spur that had snapped off his boot. He brought it up and slashed it across Rafferty's face and then sunk the knifelike rowels deep across his throat.

Fargo raked the spur across Rafferty's eyes, blinding him. Rafferty screamed and fell backward. Fargo freed himself, struggled to his feet, and then began stomping Rafferty in a way that expressed his complete hatred of the man.

He stomped him for a good long time.

21

"I was just about to get a posse together," Sheriff Culhane said.

Fargo, Culhane, and the doctor stood outside the front door. Inside, Callie was sleeping. The doc had ordered her to bed for three days and would hear no argument.

"Glad you didn't," Fargo said. "I wanted to have a little fun with Rafferty before I turned him over to you. What about the money?"

Culhane grinned. "A priest can always use money."

Fargo smiled and nodded in agreement.

"You headed anywhere special?" the doc said. "Callie'll be sorry you left town."

"Need to be going," Fargo said. "Not sure just where as yet." He grinned. "I guess I sort of make it up as I go along."

Culhane looked at the doc and smiled. "Now that's how I always wanted to live. Sort of make it up as I go along."

"Yep," the doc said. "I agree. But at my age that'd be a little rough on the rheumatism and the arthritis and the asthma."

Culhane shook Fargo's hand. "I guess he's got a point there."

"Yeah," Fargo said, "I guess he has."

A few minutes later he waved good-bye from the saddle atop his stallion. Then he was gone, heading into the starry Texas twilight.

LOOKING FORWARD!
The following is the opening
section from the next novel in the exciting
Trailsman series from Signet:

THE TRAILSMAN #281

NEW MEXICO NIGHTMARE

Northern New Mexico Territory, 1859—
Where a fire-breathing monster stalks by night,
and Fargo is both hunter and hunted.

Skye Fargo kneed his pinto stallion up out of a long cut-
bank, then drew rein. His slitted gaze swept the terrain to
make sure it was safe to skyline himself. Then he stood up
in the stirrups to ease the pressure on his saddle-sore
tailbone.

He had finally reached the end of the Cimarron cutoff,
the only northern route into New Mexico Territory that
skirted rock-strewn Raton Pass. Due west, straight ahead
of him, loomed the towering Sangre de Cristo Mountains,
with the Rio Grande valley tucked out of sight just behind
them and Santa Fe a few days ride to the southwest.

It was vastly more lush and green here than in the deso-
late landscape farther south. This was rolling foothill country, the grassy slopes dotted with towering evergreens.

Craggy-barked cottonwoods marked the banks of numerous creeks.

"Well, old campaigner, welcome to the land of Coronado," he remarked to his Ovaro. "We should make Chico Springs around sunset. Then we'll slap an oat bag on you."

Fargo's belly rumbled like an underground thermal spring. Hours earlier he'd gnawed the remainder of his last pemmican cake.

However, before he rode on, Fargo drew his Colt. He spun the cylinder with a fast, rattling click like a roulette wheel, then gave a quick puff to clear blow sand out of the Colt's action. He leathered his weapon and slipped the riding thong over the hammer. He quickly checked the magazine in his brass-frame Henry, then booted the rifle again.

A man was wise not to be lulled by the pretty vista around here. This was treacherous country where men were shot for their boots. This ancient land had been violent and dangerous long before General Kearney hoisted the U.S. flag over the territory of New Mexico.

Fargo shook the kinks out of his arms, then changed hands on the reins. As he nudged the Ovaro up to a fast trot, he especially watched the thickets, rock tumbles, and pockets of deep grass—all favored by ambushers.

However, he reached Chico Springs, without incident, just after sunset. The one-horse burg had begun as a campsite for wagon trains after they rounded Point of Rocks on the Santa Fe Trail. The only thing that had grown much, since Fargo's last visit, was the *camposanto*—the cemetery on the eastern edge of town.

As he rode in he could spot the flickering glow of *farolitas* through open doorways. There was no church, but anyplace where the walls were thick enough, niches held cheap plaster busts of the beloved saints. Fargo reined in at the livery barn on the far side of town.

"Well, God a'mighty!" exclaimed the hostler when he got a good look at the Ovaro in the oily yellow glow of a kerosene lantern. "Son, that stallion is high-grade horseflesh."

The old codger was at least sixty, with a face marked

by deep seams. But his twinkling eyes were alive with sly good humor.

Fargo was surprised when the Ovaro, usually wary around strangers, nuzzled the old man's bony shoulder. "Say . . . looks like you got a way with horses, Dad."

"I oughter. First forty years of my life, onliest time I clumb outta the saddle was to crap. The name's Hooky McGhee, and use to, I broke green horses to leather for the army. But there's cobwebs on them memories, boy."

"Rubdown and a feed," Fargo said, flipping the old-timer a four-bit piece.

Fargo nodded toward the open double doors. Across the street, an armed guard sat next to a stack of new boards. There were very few sawmills this far west, and huge freighting difficulties. Now lumber thieves were prowling the far frontier, where finished boards were at a premium.

"I see the board bandits have invaded this area, too?" Fargo asked.

"Hunh! Does a rag doll have a patched ass?"

Fargo headed toward the center of town and the only cantina, whose owner had never bothered to hang out a sign. He stepped through a doorless archway into a dimly lighted, smoky room with an earthen floor.

A Pueblo Indian wrapped in the traditional manta was placing steaming bowls down in front of two Mexicans at one of the tables. A third customer nursed a bottle of tequila at a deal counter. The place was so rustic that the chairs were simply hardtack boxes and empty packing crates.

"Muy buenas tardes, señor," the Indian owner greeted him as Fargo parked himself at the far end of the counter, so he could face the doorway. "I am Antonio Two Moons, *a sus órdenes*—at your service."

The moon-faced owner squinted slightly, studying Fargo's face closer. "You have been here before, *verdad*? Perhaps . . . two years ago?"

Fargo nodded. "That's some memory you got, Antonio."

"No, I forget many faces. But not yours. You are the gringo *famoso,* the Trailsman."

"Right now this gringo is more famished than famous."

The word "famished" confused Antonio. *"Tiene usted hambre, señor?"*

"Damn straight I have hunger. Right now I'd eat the butt out of a skunk."

"The only skunks around here, *señor*, walk on two legs, *verdad*? But I have hot beans and tortillas."

Fargo flipped a Liberty Head gold dollar onto the counter. "Trot it out, amigo."

Antonio bit the small coin to make sure it was good. " *'Sta bien, señor."*

The food was simple, but tasty and filling. Fargo washed it down with milky white pulque, the cactus liquor he preferred over tequila.

"*Señor*, will you be visiting Chico Springs long?" Antonio asked as he refilled Fargo's glass.

Fargo shook his head. "I'm pushing on to Fort Union. The post commander wants to hire me as a scout for a road-building crew."

Just as Fargo finished speaking, an Anglo male wearing a big buffalo hide coat stepped into the cantina. Fargo was instantly alerted—he'd learned from experience never to trust any man who was dressed too warm for the weather.

The man was bearing right toward him. Fargo snapped his Colt out onto the counter, holding it but not cocking the hammer.

"Care to purchase a good firearm, friend?" Fargo called out in a hail-fellow tone. "It's well used, but also well oiled."

The new arrival froze in midstep, looking confused and uncertain. Then a cunning gleam seeped into his small, dull eyes. He flashed big buck teeth.

"Might could be I do need a short-iron. Le'me see it."

Now Fargo did thumb back the hammer. "I got a better idea. First you pull that hog-grinder out from under your coat. Butt-first and *slow,* or I'll blow you to hell."

The cantina went silent like a courtroom after a confession. Those crude chairs scuffed the rammed-earth floor as patrons cleared a ballistics lane.

"Sainted backsides!" Antonio Two Moons crossed himself. "Saint Joseph, pray for us," he muttered.

The man in the hide coat hesitated. Fargo wagged the Colt for emphasis. "Right damn now, mister."

Scowling, the man slowly drew a sawed-off scattergun out from under his coat and put it on the counter. Fargo noticed both triggers were cocked.

"I wasn't planning to kill you, mister," the man muttered. "Only to get the drop on you and turn you over to the law in Springer."

Fargo broke open the gun's breech, pocketed the shells, and flung the weapon out into the street. "Why? You don't like my face?"

"*Why?* Don't try to hornswoggle me, stranger. You're tall, got a beard, and you're wearing buckskins. That's ig*zac*ly the description of the jasper that tried to rape Elena Vargas a few hours ago."

Fargo had no idea what the man meant, but he believed his story—nor did this man have the look of a casual killer.

"Next time I see you, rapist," the man added, "it'll be down a rifle barrel."

"That's mighty tall talk, coming from a coward who uses a hideout gun. A *man* wears his weapons openly."

But Fargo was only passing through, anyway, and he decided on discretion over valor.

"The first man I see step through this door behind me," he said as he backed out of the cantina, "is going to Glory."

Keeping an eye on the open doorway, the other on the dark street, Fargo headed slowly toward the livery, sticking to the shadows.

The sudden racket of panicked horses nickering froze him in midstep. Just then he whiffed the acrid stench of smoke—and a moment later, saw huge tongues of orange flame licking upward from the hayloft of the livery!

Even as Fargo broke into a mad dash, he heard a female scream of horrifying pain and agony that could only mean death. It came from the little shack next to the livery, a shack already totally engulfed in flames.

Fargo tried to approach it, but was driven back by heat so intense it singed his eyebrows. Anyone still inside was past help, but the livery wasn't yet totally ablaze. As shouts of "Fire!" and *"Fuego!"* broke out in English and Spanish,

Fargo burst through the double doors, hacking in the thick smoke.

Hooky McGhee lay dead near the first stall, his throat slashed from ear to ear. Fargo threw open the stall gates, freeing the trapped horses. The moment he burst back outside into the clear, leading his Ovaro, a voice rang out. *"There!* There's the son of a bitch that started the fire! Put at him!"

Fortunately for Fargo, Hooky hadn't yet stripped the Ovaro of tack before the old man was killed. Fargo swung into leather, wheeled his horse, and smacked the pinto's rump hard even as a hail of hot lead hummed and whiffed past his ears.

No other series has this much historical action!

THE TRAILSMAN

Available wherever books are sold or at
www.penguin.com

GRITTY HISTORICAL ACTION FROM
USA TODAY BESTSELLING AUTHOR

RALPH
COTTON

**Available wherever books are sold or at
www.penguin.com**

S909